WHEN THE WIND BLOWS...

"Shajok," she snapped at Dumarest, "has mountains. It has valleys. Places where God alone knows what is to be found. Maybe people calling themselves the Original People. Maybe communes of one kind or another. I don't know.

"I've more sense than to stick my neck in a noose. And, mister, if you'll take my advice, neither will you.

"See those pennons waving on every house in this town? When they stop waving, get under cover and fast. Get into shelter and stay there until the wind blows again."

"Why?"

"Because, mister," she said grimly, "if you don't, you'll stop being human, that's why."

G. Barr

EYE OF THE ZODIAC

E. C. Tubb

DAW BOOKS, INC.
DONALD A. WOLLHEIM, PUBLISHER

1301 Avenue of the Americas
New York, N. Y.   10019

Dedication:
For Elsie and Donald A. Wollheim

First Printing, September 1975

1 2 3 4 5 6 7 8 9

PRINTED IN U.S.A.

Chapter ONE

At night the sound was that of a monster, a feral roar which rose to the skies and was carried on the wind, a hungry growling interspersed with staccato explosions which thickened the air and left an acrid taint. At day the monster was revealed as a conglomeration of men and machines which tore into the flank of a mountain, delving deep, gutting ancient stone and pulverizing rock for the sake of the metal it contained.

A dual operation, the metal helping to pay for the pass and tunnel which would link inhabited areas, a passage which would rob the sea and sky of expensive and dangerous transport.

One day it would be completed—but Dumarest had no intention of seeing it. Already he had stayed on Tradum too long.

He stood by the door of the hut which housed fifty men, looking towards the west, seeing the fabulous glory of the sunset. Swaths of red and orange, pink and gold, streamers of purple and emerald caught and reflected by the mist of scudding cloud so that he seemed to be looking upward at the surface of some incredible ocean.

A relaxing sight, something to ease the fatigue born of eight hours continuous labor. Now he faced another shift as an extra night-guard. Hard work but added pay. Soon, he would have enough.

"Earl?" He turned as someone called. "You out there, Earl?"

Leon Harvey, young, thin, his face old before its time. He stepped from the hut, blinking, a towel over his arm. His face brightened as he saw Dumarest.

"You should have woken me," he accused. "You

know how Nyther is—once late on the job and you lose it."

"That could be a good thing."

"Why?" Stung, his pride touched, the youngster bridled. "Don't you think I can take it?"

"Can you?"

"Sure I can. I'm tired, true, but I'll get over it. It just takes getting used to. Anyway, I need the money."

Wanted, not needed, a difference Dumarest recognized if the other did not. He made no comment, stepping to where a trough stood beneath a line of faucets, stripping and standing beneath one, water laving his head and body as he twisted a control.

Cold water piped from a mountain stream, numbing but refreshing, causing goose-pimples to rise on his skin, the chill accentuating the pallor of the thin lines of old scars which marred his torso.

Shivering, his lips blue, Leon hastily rubbed himself down,

"You're tough, Earl," he said enviously. "That water's close to freezing."

Dumarest reached for his towel. In many ways Leon was a nuisance, but he could recognize the youngster's need, even be a little amused by his claim to affinity. He too had traveled, a few trips to nearby worlds, but it was more than that which had won his tolerance. The boy was star-crazed, filled with the yearning for adventure, unable to see dirt and squalor for what it really was. One day, perhaps, he would learn.

"Earl—"

"You talk too much."

"How else am I to learn." Leon watched as Dumarest dressed, wearing pants, sturdy knee-boots, a tunic long in the sleeves and fitting high around the throat. The gray plastic was scuffed in several places, the glint of buried mesh showing, metallic protection against the thrust of a knife, the rip of a claw. Reflected light from the setting sun winked from the nine-inch blade which Dumarest carefully wiped before slipping it into his right boot.

"Earl!"

"What now?"

"When we get the money—when I get it—can I go with you?"

"No."

"Why not? We could travel together. I could help you, maybe, and—why not, Earl?"

Too many reasons, none of which the youngster would understand. His very desire for companionship showed how unfitted he was to follow the way he had chosen. A man traveled faster alone. It was easier to get one berth than two. And two men would be easier to spot than one.

Dumarest said, "Forget it, Leon."

"Why? Is someone after you? Is that it, Earl? Are you in danger of some kind?"

A guess—or perhaps a comment too shrewd for comfort. Certainly too near the truth. Dumarest looked at the young face, the haggardness it revealed, the fatigue. Medical science could have made him appear younger, intensive training taught him a part to play, rewards offered and promises made. There could be a thousand like him scattered on worlds in this sector, placed where a destitute traveler would look for work, waiting, watchful, doing nothing until the time came to report to their masters.

Was Leon Harvey an agent of the Cyclan?

"Earl?"

"Nothing—I was thinking. Where is your home world?"

"Nerth. Not too far from here. I—"

"Nerth?"

"Yes. Earl, is something wrong? Your face—"

Dumarest forced himself to relax. It was coincidence, it could be nothing more. A name which held a special association. Nerth, Earth, an accident, surely. Yet hope, never dead, responded to the familiar sound. A lure, perhaps? If Leon was an agent of the Cyclan, he could have offered no greater enticement.

"Earth," said Dumarest. "You said Earth?"

"Earth?" Leon smiled. "Earl, are you crazy? Who the hell would call any planet by that name? No, I said Nerth. It's a quiet world, too quiet for me, I ran as soon as I got the chance. And I'm going to keep on running. Just as soon as I get enough for a passage I'm on my way. Right smack towards the Center. You've been there, Earl?"

"Yes."

"And you'll come with me?"

"Before we can go anywhere," said Dumarest. "We need the money."

They all needed money, the men who worked on the project, contract slaves killing themselves with labor to pay an ever-expanding debt. Men who had accepted an advance, spent money on clothes, drinks, luxury foods. They had tried to recoup by gambling and had lost. They stood in the middle of the hut, watching with envious eyes as others, luckier or more sensible, played with cash they still could call their own.

The lure of easy money, a fortunate win which would enable them to pay off what they owed, accumulate a little more, get a stake with which to beat the system. Some managed it, the majority did not. They would work until they died, the victims of speed-accentuated risks, of haste-compounded errors. Fools who had walked willingly into a trap.

Elg Sonef was not one of them. He was a big man, squat, his face seamed, the knuckles of both hands scarred, the spatulate fingers surprisingly deft as he manipulated the deck of cards. Every hut held one of his kind, the man who ran the game, who used fists and feet to collect and to maintain his monopoly.

"The more you put down the more you pick up," he droned. His voice was harsh, rasping, careless of the exhausted men trying to sleep in the double-tiered bunks. "Come on, lads, why hesitate? The canteen has a new consignment of liquor and you get paid in two days time. A little luck and you could take your pick of the seraglio. Why wait for luxuries?" Cards riffled from his fingers. "Make your bets. Even money on any choice."

The game was high, low, man-in-between, a simple game with simple rules. A cloth was spread on the table divided into three sections, each section with three parts. A card was dealt face up before each of the three main sections and players bet on whether it would be the highest, lowest or, the one between the others in value. Duplicates canceled out the middle. If all values were alike they paid high.

Sonef was playing by his own rules, ignoring relative odds and ensuring that, with all sections covered, he had a high advantage. An advantage increased by his own skillful dealing.

Dumarest watched, a little amused, wondering how the players could have been so gullible. At his side Leon said, wistfully, "Earl, we could double our stake in a few minutes with luck."

"Luck?"

"You think he's cheating?"

Dumarest was certain of it, but it was not his concern. He turned from the cluster of players and moved towards his bunk, thumbing open the small box at the head. The towel was still damp, but if he left it exposed it would be stolen. He threw it into the container and slammed it shut. It would stay that way until the lock recognized the imprint of his thumb.

"It's getting late, Leon. Let's eat."

The canteen was a crude hut filled with tables and benches, staffed with old men and cripples, a scatter of Hyead. Dumarest stepped aside as one came towards him busy with a broom. A thin, stooped figure, dressed in filthy robes tied with knotted string. A ravaged face, peaked, the eyes slotted like those of a goat. Blunt horns rose above a tangle of hair, gray shot with russet. The hands which held the broom were four-fingered claws.

Despised, degenerate, the product of wild mutations, found running like animals in the mountains by the early settlers and now used as servitors.

Cheap labor, working for discarded clothing and scraps of food, kicked, cursed, or ignored by men who were themselves little better than beasts.

Dumarest led the way to the counter, picking carefully at the food, selecting items high in protein and low in bulk. An expensive choice, but one which gave better nutritional value than the steaming chaff bought by the majority.

As they ate Leon said, "Earl, how did you know Sonef was cheating?"

"Did I say he was?"

"No, but was he?"

"You saw the way he dealt, cards face up and using no regular rotation. He was manipulating the bets, letting the low stakes win, taking the high. Once you know how to bottom-deal it's easy."

"Could you do it?"

Dumarest ignored the question. "Tell me about Nerth."

"It's a dump."

"And?"

"It's just a world, Earl. A backwater. Mostly farms, no industries, hardly any cities. Ships are rare. They only call to pick up furs and gems, and deliver tools and instruments. No one with any sense would want to go there."

"And you ran," said Dumarest quietly. "Why?"

"Why did you?" snapped Leon. "What started you on the move?" Immediately he was contrite. "I'm sorry, I guess that's none of my business. Let's just say that I was bored."

"A young man," said Dumarest. "You had a family, a home?"

"If you can call it that, yes." Leon stared down at his plate, then seemed to come to a decision. "I belonged to a commune, Earl. It lay well back in the hills and was as isolated as you could get. Maybe I'm a freak of some kind, but I couldn't accept what they had planned for me. The tests, the ritual, the arranged marriage, the duties." His laugh was bitter. "The duties. Can

you guess what they would have been? Just guarding a
lot of old records. A Keeper of the Shrine. In twenty
years, maybe, I'd have made assistant Guardian. In fifty,
I might have even become the Head. Fifty years of dust-
ing, brooding, worshipping—I couldn't face it, I had
to run."

"How?"

"I—does it matter?"

A boy, twisted, unsettled according to his fellows, a
rebel, a failure. Someone who would have planned,
waited and stolen when the time came. Something of
value which would have been sold to gain the initial
passage money—an old story and a familiar one. Only
the name held an unusual connotation. Nerth.

"You spoke of records. What were they?"

"Books, papers, I don't know." Leon shrugged at
Dumarest's expression. "I never saw them. They are
held sacred. A load of superstitious rubbish, of course,
but there it is. Once a year we had a ceremony and ev-
eryone congregated, and chanted and acted like a
bunch of fools. I'm well out of it."

Coincidence or design? If the latter, then the boy
was a good actor, if he were the boy he appeared to be.
A question which would have to be resolved and soon.
A decision made—and if he guessed wrong then his life
would be at stake.

Dumarest leaned back, studying the young face, the
eyes. Would the Cyclan have been so obvious? The
name, the talk of ancient records, a secret to be found,
an answer to be gained perhaps. The answer for which
he had searched for so long.

Nerth . . . New Earth . . . Earth—there had to be a
connection.

"Earl?" Leon had become aware of the scrutiny. "Is
anything wrong?"

"No." Dumarest rose to his feet. "We'd better get
moving. I'll join you at the hut."

"Why not go together?"

Dumarest made no answer, crossing to a vending

machine, waiting until the other had gone before filling
his pocket with bars of candy.

As usual, Nyther was in a foul mood. He stood behind his desk in the guard hut, a big man with a craggy
face and hard, unrelenting eyes. His shoulders strained
at the fabric of his uniform, a holstered laser heavy at
his waist. He nodded as Dumarest entered and crossed
to a table to collect his equipment.

To Leon he said, "You looked peaked, boy. I'm not
sure you can handle the job."

"I can handle it."

"Maybe, but I'm putting you under Nygas. If you
want to quit, now's the time."

A threat and a warning. Nygas was noted for his
ferocity. Men who slept on duty under his command
woke up screaming with shattered bones.

"I'm not quitting."

"Then get out of here." As the boy left Nyther said
to Dumarest, "I'm putting you on free-patrol, Earl.
Work the south-eastern sector. It means an increase
and a double bonus if you catch anyone stealing. I've
had a gutful of losses and it has to stop."

"More lights would help."

"More lights, more men and more equipment,"
agreed Nyther bleakly. "Given the money, there's always an answer. But we haven't got the money so it's
no use dreaming about it. Just stay alert, keep moving,
summon help if you think you need it, and remember
the bonus."

Outside night had fallen, the area illuminated by
floodlights set on pylons, swaths of brilliance cut by
paths of shadow, the face of the workings a blaze of
eye-bright glare. Men moved about it like ants, machines throbbing, diggers, loaders, trucks, making an
endless snarl.

Dumarest turned, heading towards his position, moving in shadow and noting everything he saw.

A group of men arguing, on the edge of a fight,
ready to kick and pummel.

A crane, the load swinging dangerously, carelessly held.

An overseer, yelling, his arms flailing to accentuate his orders.

And, everywhere, the signs of haste and urgency, the traces of poverty and neglect.

Of men, never of machines. The Zur-Sekulich Combine took care of their own.

The roar from the workings died a little, fading to a grating susuration as Dumarest neared the edge of the construction site. Stores and supplies stood in neat array, crates piled high, lashed and sealed, standing until needed. The ground was rough, bristling with rocks, laced with small cracks which could trap a foot and break an ankle. The pylons were fewer, the shadows wider.

Passing the last of the crates Dumarest halted, his body silhouetted against the light. For a long moment he stood clearly visible to anyone who might be watching from the surrounding darkness, then he moved to one side and rested his back against a crate.

There were ways to guard a depot and of them all, the Zur-Sekulich had chosen the most inefficient. There should have been infra-red detectors set in an unbroken ring about the area, men with light-amplifying devices on continual watch, rafts with sensors to spot any movement in the darkness. There should have been a close-mesh fence twenty feet high with special areas for the stores.

All things which cost money. Men and equipment which were unproductive and therefore undesirable. It was cheaper to use men, to send them out and, if they should be killed, where was the loss?

Dumarest had no intention of getting himself killed. He had chosen a better way.

Awhile and he moved again, standing before the light, returning to his former position. To one side, something moved.

"Man Dumarest?" The voice was thin, a bare whisper, the tones slurred, the words more a recognition signal than a question. The Hyead had good night-vision.

"Here." Dumarest took a candy bar from his pocket. "Emazet?"

"Abanact. The other could not come."

"He is well?"

"The other is dead. Hunters in the mountains—he will be mourned."

Trigger-happy fools who had blasted at a barely seen shape and who would now be boasting of their kill. Dumarest threw the candy bar at the dim figure which rose from the ground to catch it, to chew eagerly at the luxury. The rare but essential sugars the Hyead metabolism craved.

"News?"

"A whisper. Men will come to take what is not theirs."

"When?"

"Mid-way through the night. At a point where lights are few and the stores are high. Three hundred paces from where the other met you the last time you spoke."

The lower dump. Dumarest took out more candy bars, the reward for the information. He lifted the remainder up in his hand.

"Anything else? News from the city? Were men dressed in scarlet seen leaving the field?"

"By us, no."

"By any?"

"Not that we have heard."

The Hyead moved like ghosts through the town, worked at the field and in the taverns, listened to gossip casually spoken by men who considered them less than beasts. If a cyber had landed they would have known of it. Dumarest passed over the rest of the candy.

"If you hear of such men pass word to me at the canteen. The reward will be high."

"It is understood."

And then there was nothing but the darkness, the shadows, a thin wind which ruffled the tips of dry vegetation. A ghostly sound like the keen of mourning women.

Chapter TWO

Down by the lower dump the shadows were thick, the glow from the floodlights doing little to augment the ghostly starlight. The patches of darkness could already hide danger—on Tradum as on any world predators came in many guises, the most dangerous of which were men.

Dumarest slowed, his left hand reaching for the flashlight clipped to his belt, his right tensing on the club he had been issued. It was a yard of loaded wood, the end lashed to provide a grip, the tip rounded. Hard, strong, it could smash bones and pulp flesh.

Twice he had checked the area and now, if the information had been good, the thieves would be busy. Halting, his eyes searched the spaces between the stacked crates, their upper edges barely visible against the sky. Pilfering was rife, hungry men snatching at castings and components, desperate for the money they would bring, the food it would provide. Buyers were always to be found, taking no risks but making high profits.

"Brad!" The voice was an urgent whisper. "Which crate?"

"Any of them."

"This covering's tough. We should have brought a saw."

"Quit talking and get on with it."

Two men at least, and there could be more. One set high to act as a lookout, perhaps, an elementary precaution. Maybe another crouched and watchful to spot a figure moving against the glow from the workings. Dumarest had swung in a wide circle to approach the

15

spot from the darkness. He looked again at the upper edges of the stacked crates but saw nothing. But if he used the flashlight and someone was up there, he would be an easy target.

"Shen?"

"Nothing. All's clear."

Dumarest moved as he heard the rasp of metal on wood, a sudden splintering, the snap of a parting binding. The third voice had come from close to one side and he stepped towards it. A dark patch rested on the ground, a man who jerked as Dumarest dropped at his side, one hand clamping over his mouth, the fingers of the other digging into the throat, finding the carotid arteries, pressing and cutting off the blood supply to the brain. A pressure which brought swift unconsciousness.

"Shen?" The first man who had spoken grunted as he heaved something from the opened crate. "Give me a hand with this."

Dumarest rose and moved softly towards him. The other man, the one called Brad, must be facing the site. Three men working together to make a strike and a swift withdrawal. Dawn would find them well on their way to the city, too far for pursuit, their loot hidden at the first sign of a raft or hunters.

"Shen?" Dumarest saw the blur of a face. "What—"

The man was fast. He backed, one hand lifting with a hooked bar, his mouth opening to yell. Dumarest dived towards him, the club extended, the tip aimed at the throat, hitting, sending the man to double up, retching. A sudden flurry and Brad was facing him, a gun in his hand.

"Drop it!" he snapped. "The club, drop it!" He sucked in his breath as the wood hit the dirt. "Make a sound and you're dead. Elvach! Get down here. Fast!"

Four men, a big team, and at least one armed with a gun. A primitive weapon which would make a lot of noise, but would kill while doing it. The man would hesitate to use it, not wanting to give the alarm. Therefore, the other man would be coming in from behind with a more silent means of dealing death. A club or knife or strangler's cord.

Dumarest knew they didn't intend to leave him alive.

"Elvach! Hurry, damn you!"

From above came a scrape and a slither as the lookout dropped from his perch.

"What's happening? Where's Shen? What's the matter with Sley?" Elvach was small, lithe, anxious. His face was screwed up and his eyes barely visible in the puffiness of his cheeks.

"Never mind them," snapped Brad. "Take care of this guard. Move!"

"Kill him?"

"You want to be lasered down at dawn?" Brad lifted his pistol. "Having this gun will kill us all, if we're caught. Now get on with it."

"Wait a minute," said Dumarest. "We could make a deal. I've got money."

He dropped his hand to his boot, touched the hilt of the knife, lifted it, threw it underhand toward the face behind the gun. The point hit, plunged into an eye, the brain beneath. As Brad fell Dumarest turned, the stiffened edge of his hand slamming against the side of Elvach's neck, sending him helplessly to the dirt.

"Fast!" Sley, gasping for breath, stared his amazement. "He had a gun on you, finger on the trigger, and you killed him before he could pull it. You killed him."

"Do you want to follow him?"

"No, mister, I don't."

"Then stay here. Move and I'll cut you down." Dumarest jerked his knife free, wiped it clean on the dead man's clothing and tucked it back into his boot. He picked up the gun and went in search of Shen. Elvach looked up as Dumarest dumped the man at his side.

"Dead?"

"Unconscious. Are there any more of you?"

"No."

"I want the truth," said Dumarest harshly. "Who set this up?"

"Brad." Elvach sat upright, rubbing the side of his neck. "It was going to be easy, he said. Move in, a quick snatch and away. One to work and three to watch, we couldn't go wrong." He sounded bitter. "Like hell we couldn't."

"Who would buy?"

"I don't know. Brad had it fixed. Him and that damned gun." His voice changed, became a whine. "Look, mister, how about letting us go? You've gotten Brad. I've a woman lying sick, and a couple of kids close to starving. I made a mistake, sure, but I didn't know about the gun."

"You'd have killed me," said Dumarest flatly.

"No. Knocked you out, maybe, but not killed. What would be the point?"

To gain time, to avoid later recognition, to ensure their escape. They would have killed him.

Sley said, dully, "What now, mister? I suppose you're going to turn us in."

"That's right."

"Turn us in and collect the bonus, then see us lasered down at dawn. The gun'll take care of that. A smart trick which let us down. Brad should have fired and to hell with losing the loot. He was greedy. I guess we all were."

Greedy and stupid. Caught without the gun they would have been knocked around a little, interrogated, fined and set to work. A heavy fine which would hold them fast until the project had been completed, working for small wages, little better than slaves. But they would have stayed alive.

Dumarest lifted his whistle and blew three short blasts.

"So that's it," said Sley bleakly. "The end of the line. I hope you sleep well, mister. I hope you never have hunger tearing at your guts."

"Work won't kill you."

"Work? With that gun?"

"Gun?" Dumarest looked at it and, with a sudden movement, hurled it far into the surrounding darkness.

"What gun?"

For once Nyther was pleased. "Good work, Earl. A fine job. Four of the scum caught at once. A pity you had to kill one, but he'll serve as an example. Did you have to do it?"

"There were four of them," said Dumarest. "I didn't feel like taking chances."

"You had a club. You should have broken his skull and maybe smashed a knee."

"He had something, a bar. It could have been a gun."

"A natural mistake," admitted Nyther. "The light was bad and you couldn't have known. Hell, man, I'm not blaming you. It's just that a man like that could have friends. They might want to avenge him—you understand?"

Dumarest nodded, leaning back in his chair, conscious of his fatigue. It was dawn, the interior of the guard hut thick with stale air, a litter of returned equipment lying on the tables. The structure quivered to the endless roar from the workings.

"Did you get anything from the others?"

"No." Nyther opened a drawer in his desk and produced a bottle and glasses. Pouring, he handed one to Dumarest. "Any ideas?"

"Four men with a plan. And they knew just where to hit."

"You can say that again." Nyther scowled as he sipped at his whiskey. "Those crates held crystalloy components. Sold in the right place they would fetch a high price. Even if torn apart, the shammatite would be more than worth the trouble." A man grown old in security, he guessed what Dumarest was hinting. "An arrangement. Those men were working to a plan set out by a big operator. Right?"

"Maybe."

"Then why no guns?" Nyther answered his own question. "They shouldn't have needed them. Three men watching could have handled any normal guard.

And once the scum start using guns I'll have a case in order to increase the guard allocation. You were lucky, Earl, in more ways than one."

Dumarest drank, slowly, saying nothing.

"Four bonuses—you can collect the cash immediately. No guns and the chance of a promotion. Interested?"

"I might be."

"I've been watching you, Earl. You're wasted at the workings. Any foot can handle a machine, but it takes a special kind of man to make a good security officer. He has to have a feel for the job, an instinct. You have it. It sent you to the right place at the right time. I need all the men I can get like you."

"So?"

"How about becoming a full-time guard? I'll make you the head of a sector. Twice as much as you're getting now with free board and lodging. A deal?"

It was tempting, and it would be a mistake to refuse too quickly. A sign of guilt, perhaps. At the workings men did not hestitate at the chance of extra pay.

"Of course, I'll have to check you out with Head Office," continued Nyther. "But that's just a formality. All they want is that you be registered in the computer. The doc can take your physical characteristics and do the rest of it. A blast in the shoulder—nothing to worry about."

Dumarest set down his empty glass, watched as it was refilled.

"A radioactive trace?"

"Sure, just a precaution and, as I said, nothing to worry about. If you take off without warning, we'll know where to look for you."

The Zur-Sekulich and others who might be interested. Once branded he would stand out in any crowd, electronic tracing gear picking up the implanted pattern.

Nyther said, "I'll fix it for noon. I'll send word to your foreman to release you. By dusk you'll be ready for full-time duty. Health, Earl!"

Dumarest responded to the toast. Without knowing it, the guard chief had forced his decision. By noon he would have to be on his way.

Casually he said, "I'm grateful, Chief. Maybe I could do something for you. Are you willing to gamble an extra bonus?"

"A deal? Hell, Earl, once you start working for me—"

"I'm not working for you, Chief. Not yet, and a man has to get what he can, right?" Dumarest didn't wait for an answer. "For an extra bonus I'll tell you how to seal this place so no scavenger will have a chance. And all it will cost you is a few boxes of candy a day."

Nyther was shrewd. "The Hyead?"

"The bonus?"

"Yours, damn it. Take me for an idiot and you'll return it double." Nyther frowned as Dumarest explained. "Have they the brains for the job? Are they reliable?"

"They don't need brains just to watch and listen and the candy will keep them on the job. Arrange a meeting with one called Abanact—better still I'll do it for you. Put off the doc until tomorrow."

A day gained if the other agreed. As Nyther nodded Dumarest continued, "I'll need some candy, you can give me a chit for that, and some super-sonic whistles. We can work out a simple code so they can give you the warning without alarming the thieves. Once arranged, you can cut down on the extra guards and use regular mobile patrols."

"And if it doesn't work?"

"You get the bonus back-double."

Nyther reached for the bottle. "Now why the hell couldn't I have thought of that? The Hyead—cheap and the damned things go everywhere. You've got a point, Earl."

One he had overlooked, familiarity breeding contempt.

"The bonus," reminded Dumarest. "I'll take it now."

He collected it all in cash, thick coins which weighted down his pocket, his eyes thoughtful as he walked from the cashier's office. It was time to disappear, to vanish like a stone thrown into water, to move on before it was too late.

He could catch a lift into the city, hope for a quick passage, hide if he had to wait. For a lone man it would be simple. Nyther would be annoyed, but he had received value for his money and would quickly forget. A casual worker who had turned down the offer of a good job—why be concerned when there were so many others to take his place? And, if he had the sense to contact the Hyead, his worries would be over.

The problem was the boy. Dumarest thought about him as he moved towards his hut. Caution dictated that he keep going, head for the road and flag a truck, bribe the driver if he had to, but in any case to keep moving. No one would bother him and no one would argue. Leon, Nyther, the whole mess and approaching danger of the works could be forgotten.

But the boy had not lied? Nerth—the name was a bait. A chance he could not afford to miss. Even if the planet offered but a single clue he had to find it. Find the location of the planet of his birth. His home world. Earth!

And, to find Nerth, he needed the boy. The name was too similar. Someone, somewhere would have heard of it, and yet it appeared in none of the almanacs he had studied. A mystery which had to be resolved.

He sensed the tension as soon as he entered the hut. A crowd was clustered around the table, men who should have been sleeping remaining awake, responding to the excitement, the mounting desperation. A sure sign that big stakes were being wagered, that someone had lost all restraint.

A man turned as Dumarest touched his shoulder. His face was flushed, annoyed.

"Earl, thank God you're here. The kid's in trouble."

"Leon? What happened? Why did he play?"

"Nygas caught him dozing on duty. He broke a couple of ribs, I think. Anyway, he kicked him off the job. We strapped him up but he's unfit to work. I guess he hoped to make a stake." The man scowled. "Against Elg Sonef that's asking for a miracle. The kid doesn't stand a chance."

Leon sat at the board, sweating, his face strained, his eyes distraught as he stared at the small heap of coins remaining in his pile. Sonef's voice was a rasping purr.

"You lose again, son. Too bad. Better luck the next time. What'll you take, high, low or man-in-between?"

"I—" Leon broke off as Dumarest reached down and covered his few coins. "Earl!"

"You want in?" The gambler was unruffled. Big, unrestrained in his violence, he was fearless. "You!" He pointed at one of the players. "Move over. Make room for a real man. Cash down, Earl. Let's go!" He poised the cards.

"No."

"You don't want to play?"

"Not this game. It's for kids. Let's try something else. Poker."

"House dealing?"

"Do I look stupid?" Dumarest met the other's eyes. "We deal in turn, no limit, five card draw."

Sonef said, dangerously, "Are you saying there's something wrong with the deal?"

"Did I say that?" Dumarest shrugged. "Of course, if you're scared—"

"Like hell I'm scared!" The big man bristled. "You name it and I'll play it."

He'd been pressured and must have known it, but was unable to refuse the challenge. Big and tough though he was, previous losers could bear grudges and it took little strength to slip a blade into a sleeping man. He grunted as Dumarest sat, heaping coins before him, the glitter of his accumulated bonuses.

"Anyone else want to sit in?"

Two men accepted the invitation followed by a third, a pale man with slender hands who rarely played. Dumarest gave him one glance, recognized him for

what he was and made his own, mental reservations.
The two would play in partnership, operating a squeeze
and manipulating the deal. Against them a normal
player would have no chance.

Dumarest was not a normal player. Too often during
the tedious journeys between the stars he had run the
tables in the salons, providing a means to beguile the
passengers traveling on High passage. These were the
men and women drugged with quicktime, the magic
compound which slowed their metabolisms so that, to
them, hours passed as quickly as minutes. And there
had been others, gamblers who had become friends and
who had taught him the tricks of their trade.

Even so, it took time. The cards had to be stacked,
the backs marked with slight indentations of a nail, a
trick which if noticed by the others would be put down
to each other. And the system of play had to be recognized and used against those who employed it.

Sonef was the lesser of the two, Lekard dangerously
skillful. The other men were padding, caught up by the
excitement, limited as to resources and quickly disposed of. Dumarest used them, adding to his pile,
throwing in good hands when he knew that Sonef or
Lekard would have given themselves better. Cautious
play, as he waited for the moment he knew was sure to
come.

Sonef grunted as the three were left in sole possession of the table. "Now we can really get down to it.
Your deal, Lekard."

The moment, Dumarest was certain of it. He
watched as the cards fell, picked up his hand and
looked at it. Three aces, a nine, and a deuce.

"I'll open."

Sonef was to his left. "I'll just double that, Earl.
Lekard?"

"I'll stay."

Not an obvious squeeze play, then, but that would
come later. Dumarest met the raise and raised in turn.
Sonef doubled, Lekard stayed, Dumarest raised again
and was raised by Sonef. Lekard dropped out.

It was between the two of them, and Dumarest knew exactly what was intended. He frowned at his cards, apparently uncertain, a man tempted but a little afraid.

"Earl?"

Dumarest looked at his money. "I'll raise," he said. "All of it. Table stakes, right?"

"No limit, Earl, that was what we agreed."

From the circle of watchers a man growled, "What the hell, Sonef, aren't you ever satisfied? You trying to buy the pot or what?"

Draw poker, no limit. A man with enough money would always win because he could put down more than his opponent could match. A risk Dumarest had taken, one lessened now that Lekard had dropped out. He could match the other's bet, but after? He knew what would happen after.

"Table stakes," said another man from among the watchers. "We always play that way. No limit, but you can't beat a man into the ground. I say meet his pile, draw, and show."

"You're not playing," snapped the gambler. "So you just shut your mouth. Earl, if you want I'll accept your paper. Good enough?"

I.O.U's which would carry a high rate of interest. Registered with the company cashier, Dumarest would be working for the gambler until the debt was paid. Again he pretended to hesitate.

"Any amount?"

"As high as you want. And I'll meet it with cash." Sonef, certain he would win, could afford to be generous. "Hell, Earl, shove in the cash and I'll match it. Then we can draw. Fair enough?

Dumarest nodded, waited until the money was placed, and looked again at his hand. Three aces. No normal player would do other than draw two cards hoping for a pair, or a fourth ace.

He said, "Put down the deck, Lekard."

"What?"

"Put it down." Steel flashed as Dumarest lifted his knife and slammed the point through the pasteboards into the table beneath. To a man standing at his side he said, "Pull them from the top. I want no seconds or bottoms—just deal them as they come."

The man was uncertain. "Elg?"

"Do it." Sonef was confident. "Just deal them as he says. How many do you want, Earl?"

Dumarest dropped the nine, the deuce and one of the aces. "I'll take three."

He heard the incredulous suck of breath from a man behind him, a kibitzer who had seen his hand, saw the sudden hardening of Sonef's face, the accentuated pallor on Lekard's thin features.

He didn't have to look at his cards, he knew what they had to be. An ace followed by two cards of the same suit, either of which would have completed Sonef's running flush. If he had taken one card or two, he would have held four aces against a winning hand.

He said, flatly, "I bet a hundred. You want to see me? No? Then I've won."

He rose, dropping his cards face upwards, sweeping the money into his pocket. To Leon he said, "Get your gear. It's time for us to go."

Chapter THREE

They reached the city at mid-afternoon, dropping from the raft which had carried them, the driver waving a casual farewell as he drifted away. The area was bleak, a mass of warehouses and rugged ground, huts and offices showing hasty construction. An extension of the old town which lay in a hollow, at the head of a strait leading to the sea.

The field lay beyond on a stretch of leveled ground, ringed with a high perimeter fence topped with floodlights. On Tradum the authorities maintained a check on all arrivals and departures, a policy backed by the Zur-Sekulich as a precaution against contract-workers leaving before their time.

Leon said, "What now, Earl?"

"We find somewhere to stay. Then we eat, then I'll look around."

"Can't I come with you?"

"No, you'd better rest those ribs."

"Nygas!" The boy scowled. "That animal! He had no right—"

"You were warned," said Dumarest curtly. "You knew what to expect."

He glanced at the sky. Walking would save money, but be costly in time. He waved as a pedcar came into sight, the operator a slender man with grotesquely developed thighs. Leon sighed with relief as he slumped into the open compartment at the rear. His face was pinched, the nostrils livid, dark shadows around his eyes. He clutched a small bag, the sum total of his possessions, a cheap thing of soiled fabric which he rested

on his lap. Dumarest had nothing aside from what he
carried on his person.

"Peddling," the operator asked, "You from the workings? I ask because I was thinking of getting a job up
there. A friend of mine, my sister's second cousin, he
reckons a man could do real well. You think it's worth
me trying?"

"No harm in that."

"I could handle a machine given the chance. And I
can take orders—hell, in this job you do it all the time.
Say, you boys looking for a little excitement?"

Dumarest said, dryly. "What had you in mind?"

"There's a new joint opened on Condor Avenue.
Young girls, sensatapes, analogues, all the drinks you
can handle, and all the games you can use. Fights too,
if you're interested. Real stuff, no messing about, naked
blades and no stopping. Interested?"

They were from the workings. Men from a long bout
of hard, relentless labor would be interested.

"Condor Avenue," said Dumarest. "What's it
called?"

"The Effulvium. Crelk Sugari runs it. If you want,
mister, I'll take you straight there. Why waste time?"
His chuckle was suggestive. "Get in while the fruit is
unspoiled, eh?"

"We'll drop in later."

"You do that." The operator handed back a card.
"Hand this in when you arrive. It'll get you a free
drink. A big one, and you won't have to pay entry.
Don't forget now."

Dumarest took the slip of pasteboard. Handed in, it
would ensure the man his commission.

"You know a good hotel? Something not too high
and with available service?"

"Service?" The man twisted his head, grinning. "I
get it. Sure, Madam Brandt runs a nice, clean, interesting place. Just don't make too much noise and everything will be fine. You want me to take you there?"

"Just drop us close by. You got a card for me to give
her? Thanks."

Leon staggered a little as he left the pedcar, leaning on Dumarest for support as the vehicle moved away, the operator waving and pointing to the front of a house with shuttered windows and gaudy streaks of paint on the walls.

Dumarest watched him go, then turned and headed in the other direction.

"Aren't we going in there, Earl?"

"No."

"But I thought—" Leon frowned. "That man thinks we'll stay there."

"Which is why we won't." Dumarest stared at the pale face. "Can you hold up until we find somewhere else?"

"I guess so." Leon made an effort to stand upright. "I guess I'll have to."

"That's right," said Dumarest. "You do."

He settled for a small place in a quiet street, run by a woman long past her prime. The room had twin beds, a washbasin and faucet, a faded carpet on the floor, frayed curtains at the window. The panes were barred and faced a narrow alley. The walls were cracked and the ceiling stained. From a room lower down the passage came the sound of empty coughing.

"Chell Arlept," she explained. "He worked with my husband up at the site. They got caught in an explosion. Chell ruined his lungs. My husband—" She broke off, swallowing.

"It happens," said Dumarest. "I'm sorry."

"They just left him there," she said bleakly. "Piled dirt over the place where he fell. I didn't even get compensation."

Dumarest said nothing.

"I'm sorry. I didn't mean to tell you, but you did ask about Chell. If there's anything you need?"

"I'll let you know," said Dumarest. "There's a bath at the end of the passage? Good." He looked pointedly at the door. As the woman left he said to the boy. "Get stripped. I want to look at those ribs."

Nygas had been savage, or perhaps he had misjudged his victim. Leon winced as Dumarest's fingers probed his side, the strappings that had been hastily applied lying to one side on the bed. One rib was broken, others cracked, the flesh ugly with bruises.

"How bad is it, Earl?"

"Bad enough." Dumarest picked up the bandages, soaked them in water from the faucet, bound them tightly around the slender torso. "Just lie there and get some sleep. Don't move unless you have to and, when you do, don't bend. Hungry?"

"I could eat."

"I'll get the woman to bring you a meal. If she wants to feed you, don't argue."

"You leaving, Earl?"

Dumarest smiled at the look of concern. "Don't worry, Leon. I'll be back."

Finding the hotel had taken time, taking care of the boy still more. It was dusk as Dumarest neared the heart of the city, the square where the market was located. Beyond it lay the wharves from which boats were already putting out to fish the turbulent seas. Around it, running along the avenues to either side, were the palaces of pleasure, the casinos, dream parlors, brothels, the places in which men could pander to their inclinations. Establishments for the rich, or those with money to burn. The market was for the poor.

Beggars were prominent, men with crippled limbs and scarred faces, discarded veterans of mercenary wars. They jostled women selling dubious pleasures, others offering lucky charms, vials of aphrodisiacs, pods of narcotic seeds. In the market proper, traders displayed their wares on stalls illuminated by brightly colored lanterns which fought the encroaching darkness with pools of red and green, yellow and amber, pale blue and nacreous white.

In the kaleidoscope of brilliance heaps of tawdry jewelry, gaudy fabrics, and cheap adornments looked like rare treasure stolen from fabled temples.

A crone called out as Dumarest passed where she sat before a table brilliant with cabalistic symbols.

"Your fortune, my lord? Told with skills won from an ancient race and passed down through seventeen generations. Learn of the dangers which may lie in your path, perils which can be avoided."

Another swung a small bag suspended from a gilded chain which, she assured him, would give full protection against the diseases of love, poisoned waters, and wild radiation.

A man sat like a brooding idol over an assembly of finger rings holding vibrant darts, needles tipped with venom, artificial fingernails of razor-sharp steel, brooches which could blast a stunning gas; subtle mechanisms for dealing death and pain, things much used by the harlots who needed such protection.

Dumarest paused at a stall from which rose tantalizing odors, buying a skewer of meat and vegetables seared over a flame. The food was hot, pungent with spice, crisp to the tongue. The woman who served him was tall, darkly attractive, the cleft in her blouse doing little to hide the swell of her breasts.

She watched as he ate with the fastidious neatness of a cat, her eyes roving over his face, his body, noting the tall hardness of him, the instinctive wariness. A man who had learned to survive the hard way, she decided. One without the protection and benefit of Guild, House or Organization. His face was somber, the planes and contours revealing an inner determination, the mouth hovering on the edge of becoming cruel. He met her eyes as he dropped the empty skewer on a tray.

"You like it?"

"It was good," he admitted. "How's trade?"

"It's early yet." She turned to stare at the Hyead who worked at the back of the stall. "Better start another batch, Kiasong. Set them up and leave them to soak." To Dumarest she said, "He's willing but he has to be watched."

"And comes cheap?"

She shrugged, quivers manifest beneath the thin material of her blouse, the breasts, unbound, moving like oiled balloons.

"I give him food and a place to sleep. I had a man once, but he wanted more than I was willing to give. Now I operate alone." Pausing she added, deliberately, "Maybe, if he had looked like you things would have been different."

Dumarest smiled at the compliment.

"Well, that's the way it goes," she said. "You looking for something?"

"A healer."

"You sick?" She shrugged again as he made no answer. "Try Bic Wan, he's two rows over, three stalls down. Not the cheapest, but you can trust his goods. Tell him Ayantel sent you, he'll treat you fair."

He was a small man, wizened, his eyes like jewels in the meshed contours of his face. A round hat hugged his skull and his hands were thin, the fingers long, the nails sharpened to points. He sat behind a display of vials and containers of tablets and pills. Bunches of dried herbs hung beside clusters of seeds, withered fruits, strands of sun-dried kelp. A skull bore a tracery of lines, hollow sockets staring at the crowd. Metal chimes made small tinklings in the rising breeze.

"Ayantel," he said. "A fine woman with a shrewd mind and a discerning eye. She guided you well. What are your needs?" He blinked as Dumarest told him. "The salve I can supply, the bone mender also, together with a syringe. But the other? My friend, what you ask is not easy."

Dumarest produced coins, let them fall from one hand to the other.

"A compound to erase the barrier between truth and falsehood—how often have husbands asked for the same? Deluded men and suspicious women, eager to quell their fears or discover their rivals. If I had such a thing my fortune would be made."

"Then you can't help me?"

"My friend, I am honest with you. I could give you what seems to do as you wish, but the resultant babble would be meaningless, the product of hallucination. You wish advice?"

"I am always willing to learn."

"A wise man, and a humble one. That is well. Many would throw it back in my face and therefore compound their stupidity. There are means to induce sleep and, when used, there is a period during which questions may be asked and will be answered. It will not last long and the drug can only be used once. There are better methods, but they are the prerogative of the authorities. I am only a poor man, a seller of salves and healing compounds, what would I know of such things?" His shrug, his gesture, were timeless.

"Give me what you can," said Dumarest.

He turned as the old man busied himself with items taken from beneath his counter. The market was growing busy, the scattered wanderers reenforced by workers from the field, others on leave from the site. Locals too, gaily dressed men and girls seeking recreation. From one side came the steady beating of a drum, the wail of a flute, a troupe of dancers spinning, flesh glowing in the multicolored illumination. Cunningly they stooped to pick up thrown coins, each gesture a titivation.

Life, brash, gay, abandoned, ruled the market square. It would grow to a crescendo, peaking at midnight when the stalls closed, the revellers wending their way home, others moving on to more decadent pursuits.

Against them, the monk stood like a faded statue in somber brown.

He stood before the exchange, an ornate building facing the square in which fortunes were made and lost, merchants gambling on cargoes which had yet to arrive. He was tall, thin. The face shielded by the cowl was emaciated with deprivation. A beggar without pride and having little success. The chipped bowl of plastic in his hand was empty. The sandals on his bare feet were scuffed, a strap broken and held together with twine. His voice was a droning murmur.

"Of your charity, brother, remember the poor."

Few looked, less lingered, none threw money into the bowl. A plump trader, his hands heavy with gems, his face oiled with good living, laughed as he flung a harlot a coin.

"That for your smile, Mayelle. Today I cleared a big profit. Tomorrow—who can tell?"

"Thank you, my lord." Deftly the coin was slipped beneath a gown slit to reveal glimpses of what lay beneath. "If a smile brought so much, then surely a kiss would bring more?"

"Don't tempt me, girl. I cannot afford the delay. Even while talking a fortune could be made."

"Brother," said the monk, "remember the poor."

"You remember them." The plump man was indifferent. "I'm too busy."

Brother Saire made no comment, felt no anger at the cynicism. To have done so would have been to verge on the sin of pride, and that would have been a refutation of what he was and what he stood for. Pride and self-indulgence had no place in the Church of the Universal Brotherhood. Each monk shed all thought of personal comfort when he donned the plain, homespun robe, took the bowl of plastic, accepted the privation which would be his normal lot.

A hard life, but none who joined the Brotherhood expected otherwise. To stand, to beg, to give aid when aid could be given, to comfort always. To follow the creed of the Church, to extend the teaching which alone would end all hurt, all pain, all despair. No man is an island. All belong to the *corpus humanitatis*. The anguish of one is the torment of all. If all men could be brought to recognize one basic truth, to remember as they looked at another—*there, but for the grace of God, go I*—the millennium would have arrived.

"Of your charity, brother, remember the poor."

Halting before the monk Dumarest said, "Brother, I need your help."

"You are in distress?"

"No." Dumarest dropped coins in the bowl. He was generous, but both knew it was not a bribe. "I need information."

"There are places where answers may be found."

Taverns, shops, agencies, the field itself, the records, the complex which sold computer-time, the men who traded in nothing else. But each question would leave a trail, arouse curiosity, focus unwanted attention on him.

"There is a young man," said Dumarest. "A boy. Leon Harvey. I wondered if you know of him."

"Does he belong to the Church?"

"I don't know. Maybe."

"A casual?"

It was possible. A young man, on the run, lonely and perhaps afraid. The Church would have offered him comfort and more. The bread of forgiveness given to all who sat beneath the benediction light when, hypnotized, they eased their souls and suffered subjective penance. There were many who joined the queues for the sake of the wafer of concentrate. The monks regarded it as a fair exchange—food in return for the instilled conditioning which made it impossible to kill. The reason Dumarest had never sat beneath the light.

He said, "Leon is a runaway. He might have been reported and your aid sought."

"A boy, one of so many, how would we know of him?"

"You know, Brother. We both know."

By means of the hyper-radio incorporated into each benediction light. Monks were everywhere, tolerated and befriended by those in high places, in constant touch with the great seminary on Hope. And a parent, desperate, would have asked for help, or at least eased their hearts to listening ears. A small hope, but one which had to be followed.

Dumarest was not disappointed when, after a moment, the monk shook his head. "We have been asked to look for no one of that name. Where did he originate?"

"Nerth. You know it?"

"An odd name—no, I have no knowledge of any such world. The boy, of course, could be lying. You have considered the possibility?"

"Yes."

"Your name?"

Dumarest gave it, adding, "I am not unknown to the Church. If Brother Jerome was still alive he would vouch for me, but you can check the records."

"There is no need." The monk's eyes were direct. "As you say, you are known. If I could help you I would, but that does not seem possible. However, there is one thing perhaps you should know. Cyber Hsi has landed on Tradum."

Chapter FOUR

Manager Loh Nordkyn was disturbed. His reports had always been on time, work was progressing according to schedule, and the powers ruling the Zur-Sekulich had no reason for dissatisfaction, yet they had sent a cyber to Tradum.

He was housed in an upper suite of the company building, the windows giving a fine view of the town and space field, a view which meant nothing to Hsi as he sat at a desk studying the mass of data provided by the manager's aides.

He was tall, thin, robed as were the monks of the Universal Brotherhood, but there the similarity ended. He wore, not brown homespun, but scarlet fabric of fine weave, the Seal of the Cyclan prominent on his breast. His head was shaved, accentuating the skull-like appearance of the deep-set eyes, the skin drawn taut over bone. A living machine of flesh and bone and blood, all capacity for emotion eradicated by training and an operation performed during his youth, his only pleasure that of mental achievement.

A man who had dedicated his life to the pursuit of coldly logical reason. One to whom food was a tasteless fuel. A creature who could take a handful of facts and build a sequence of events from them culminating in a predicted eventuality.

He glanced up as the door opened, leaning back in his chair, his eyes watchful.

"Manager Nordkyn." The inclination of his head was perfunctory. "It is late. I had not thought to see you until tomorrow."

"I was curious," admitted the manager. "To to frank,

I cannot understand why the company should have chosen to employ the services of the Cyclan. We have our own computers and the operation programs are proving successful."

"As yet, perhaps."

"A trend?" Nordkyn frowned. "I have run a complete series of analogues and have found nothing to pose any serious problems."

"And perhaps none will be found." Hsi touched the sheets before him, the reams of data, incidents, reports all compressed into symbolic language. "However, I notice that your progress per man-hour is falling."

"A seam of adamantine rock which delayed progress," said Nordkyn quickly. "It was anticipated and, now that we have penetrated it, lost time will be regained."

"Casualties seem to be high."

"Carelessness due to untrained labor. We are operating under a tight cost-schedule, as you must know. But is is unimportant, men are cheap." He added, incredulously, "Surely the Zur-Sekulich are not concerned over the loss of a few vagrants?"

"No."

"Then, with respect, I fail to see what you can achieve."

"You doubt the efficiency of the Cyclan?" Hsi's voice was a smoothly modulated monotone devoid of all irritant factors, yet Nordkyn was swift to refute the accusation.

"No! Of course not!"

"But you fail to see what can be gained by my advice." Hsi touched the sheets again, selected one. "Let me illustrate. Due to the price rise in basic staples, the food served at the canteens has fallen in terms of nutritional value to a factor of fifteen percent during the past eight weeks. This has resulted in a loss of physical energy and therefore, a lessening of productive effort put out by the workers. The financial gain is more than lost by reduced efficiency. If it is continued there will be an increase in accidents and deaths. There will also be a higher incidence of sickness and minor injury. Unless there is a change I predict that, within two months, you will be three and a half days behind schedule. This prediction is in the order of 89.6 percent of probability."

"I see." Nordkyn was thoughtful. "In that case you suggest—"

"I suggest nothing," said Hsi evenly. "I give no orders and insist on no change. I merely tell you what will be the most probable outcome of any series of events. What action you choose to take is entirely your own concern."

And, if he failed, his career would be over. Nordkyn didn't need to have it spelled out in detail. The Zur-Sekulich had no time for failure.

He said, "I will order the food to be changed at once. The expense will be high, but I'll manage somehow." Hesitating he added, "Is there anything else?"

"For the moment, no."

"Then I'll leave you, Cyber Hsi." Nordkyn backed toward the door, sweating. He was glad to leave the room.

Hsi turned again to the papers. Things were going as planned. The manager was a fool, concerned only with the job in hand. The Zur-Sekulich little better, thinking only of immediate profit, the wealth of the reclaimed metal, the subsidy they won from the Tradum authorities, dreaming of the constant stream of profits they would collect from tools once the passage was completed.

Later he would visit the Tradum Council, seek out those with the greatest powers, sow seeds of dissatisfaction in the minds of the landowners, those who now operated the sea and air transports.

Faced with ruin they would cooperate, forming a cabal to seize power, relying on the Cyclan to show them how to take and hold it. And then, once they were established, the pattern set, others would move in. Tools of the Cyclan, leaders willing to obey, men eager to be guided.

And yet another world would have fallen under the domination of the organization of which he was a part.

Already the hidden power of the Cyclan reached across the galaxy, worlds secretly manipulated by resident cybers, all living extensions of Central Intelligence, all working to a common end. The complete and total domination of all humanity everywhere.

Hsi turned a sheet, scanned it, his brain absorbing, assessing, collating the information it contained. A mass of trivia, yet each item could be part of something greater, each detail a step in a logical series of events.

"Master!" His acolyte entered the chamber at the touch of a bell. "Your orders?"

"Contact Chief Nyther at the workings. He reported a small gang of pilferers were captured. One was killed with a thrown knife. Find out who did it." A moment and it was done.

"Master, the man concerned was Earl Dumarest. He—"

Dumarest! Hsi rose and stepped towards the inner room. It was soft with unaccustomed luxury, the couch covered with silk, the mattress like a cloud.

"Total seal," he ordered. "I am not to be disturbed for any reason whatsoever."

As the door closed behind him, he touched the bracelet locked around his left wrist. From the device came an invisible field which ensured that no electronic eye or ear could focus on the vicinity. A precaution, nothing more, it would defy an electronic genius to probe the ability he possessed.

Relaxing on the couch, he closed his eyes and concentrated on the Samatachazi formulae. Gradually he lost sensory perception, the sense of touch, taste, smell and hearing, all dissolved into a formless blur. Had he opened his eyes he would have been blind. Locked in the confines of his skull his brain ceased to be irritated by external stimuli. It became a thing of reasoning, awareness, and untrammeled intellect. Only then did the grafted Homochon elements become active.

Rapport was established. Hsi became fully alive.

Each cyber had a different experience. For him, it was as if he drifted in an infinity of scintillant bubbles which burst to shower him with incredible effulgence. Spheres which touched to coalesce, to part, to veer in diverse paths, to meet again in an intricate complex of ever-changing patterns. Patterns of which he was an integral part, immersing himself in the effulgence and, by so doing, becoming both a part of and one with the whole.

Like a skein of dew the spheres stretched to all sides. Brilliant, shimmering, forming a moving, crystalline pattern, at the heart of which rested the headquarters of the Cyclan.

The Central Intelligence which made contact, touching, absorbing his knowledge as a sponge would suck water from a puddle. Mental communication of incredible swiftness.

"Dumarest?"

Agreement.

"Probability of error? Predictions low on possibility of his being on Tradum. Basis for assumption?"

Explanation.

"Probability high. Variable factor of deliberate random movement negates previous predictions. Take all steps to ensure that Dumarest is apprehended. Utmost priority. Of most urgent importance that he is not allowed to escape. Full protective measures to be employed at all times."

Understanding.

"Successful culmination will result in advancement. All previous instructions canceled. Find and hold Dumarest."

The rest was sheer mental intoxication. There was always a period after rapport, during which the Homochon elements sank back into quiescence. The physical machinery of the body began to realign itself with mental affinity, but the mind was assailed by ungoverned impacts. Hsi floated in an ebon void, experiencing strange memories and unknown situations—fragments of overflow from other minds, the discard of a conglomerate of intelligences. The backwash of the tremendous cybernetic complex which was the heart of the Cyclan.

One day he would be a part of it. His body would weaken, his senses grow dull, but his mind would remain active. Then he would be taken, his brain removed from his skull, immersed in a nutrient vat, hooked in series to the countless others which formed Central Intelligence.

There he would rest, wait, and work to solve all the problems of the universe. Every cyber's idea of the ultimate paradise. Find and hold Dumarest and it would be his.

Leon stirred, sweating. "Earl! That hurts!"

"Not for long." The salve was a sticky paste which vanished into the skin beneath Dumarest's fingers. A numbing compound smelling of peat and containing the juice of various herbs. A crude anesthetic which would ease the pain of bruises and diminish the nagging agony of the broken rib. "Steady now."

"Earl?"

"Steady—move and you'll break the needle."

A hypogun would have been more efficient, blasting its charge through skin and fat and flesh, but the syringe would have to do. Dumarest rested his hands on the boy's side, feeling the ends of the broken rib, hearing the sudden inhalation, the barely stifled cry. Quickly he set the bone and, lifting the syringe, thrust the needle home. Leon convulsed as the tip hit bone.

"Hold still, damn you!"

Harsh words, but they did as intended. Pride held the boy still as Dumarest fed the hormone-rich compound from the syringe into the area around the broken rib. It would hold, seal and promote rapid healing. The thing done, Dumarest threw aside the empty syringe and rebound the slender torso.

"You do nothing for the next three days," he said flatly. "You lie there, you eat and you sleep, and that's all. Understand?"

Leon lifted a hand and wiped sweat from his eyes. In the dim light from the single bulb, he looked ghastly pale.

"And you?"

"Never mind me—we're talking about you. That rib will heal if left alone. Try and act the hero and you'll lacerate a lung and wind up dead, or in hospital." Dumarest picked up the third item which the package given him by Bic Wan had contained. A wrinkled pod which, squeezed, would release a puff of spores. A narcotic dust which would bring sleep and, he hoped, a loose and honest tongue.

"Earl, we're traveling on together, aren't we?"

"Maybe."

A lie, but a vague one. When he moved on, Dumarest intended to be alone. Crossing the room he looked through the window. The alley was in thick shadow, vagrant beams of illumination touching walls, a shuttered window, a can of garbage. From down the hall came the monotonous sound of coughing, as Chell Arlept waited for the panacea of sleep. Money could have cured him, given him fresh lungs grown from tissues of the old, but he had no money.

"Earl?"

"Your home world," said Dumarest slowly. "What made you say it was Nerth?"

"Because it is."

"You know how to get back there?"

"I don't want to go back." Leon eased himself on the bed. "I never want to see it again. I managed to get away and I'm staying away."

"Tell me," said Dumarest. "Does it have a large, silver moon? Is the sky blue at day and thin with stars at night?"

"It's got a moon," admitted the boy. "And, yes, a blue sky. The stars are thin too, but that's because it's a long way from the Center. Just like they are here. Why, Earl? What's your interest?"

Dumarest said, "Lean back. Make yourself comfortable. Close your eyes, that's it. Now breathe deeply,

deeply, good." Lifting the pod he squeezed it, gusting a fine spray at the boy's mouth, seeing the minute spores enter the nostrils to be absorbed by the inner membranes.

Within seconds he was asleep.

"Leon, listen to me." Dumarest dropped to his knees beside the narrow bed. "Answer me truthfully—have you ever heard of the Cyclan?"

"No."

"Did anyone tell you to speak to me, to mention Nerth?"

"No."

"Is there such a place, or did you make up the name because you were afraid of something?"

"Nerth," murmured the boy. "No! I won't!"

"Steady!" He quieted beneath Dumarest's hand. "What made you run?"

"I—they, no! No, I won't do it!"

"Do what? Answer me, Leon, do what?"

The boy shifted on the bed, sweat shining on his face, his voice deepening, taking on the pulse of drums.

"From terror they fled to find new places on which to expiate their sins. Only when cleansed will the race of Man be united again."

The creed of the Original People. Dumarest rose, staring down at the bed, the figure it contained. A boy, too young to know what he was saying, or someone primed for just such an eventuality. The drug he'd used was primitive—any biological technician could have provided conditioning against it, primed the youngster with intriguing answers to appropriate questions.

Any information he could give would be valueless, and already he was convinced the boy had lied.

A knock and he spun as the door swung open.

"What—?" The woman was middle-aged, dowdy, her face seamed, relieved only by the luminosity of her eyes. Wide now as they stared at Dumarest's face, the glitter of the naked blade in his hand.

He spoke before she could scream. "What do you want?"

"The boy—I heard that he was ill. I wondered if I could help?"

"Are you a nurse?" Dumarest sheathed the knife.

"Yes, in a way. I work at the hospital and try to help others in my spare time. Chell Arlept, you know of him?"

"The dying man? Yes."

"I call sometimes. There's not much I can do, but at least I can help him to sleep. I wondered—"

"What I was doing with a knife in my hand?" Dumarest smiled, casually at ease. "You startled me, that's all."

"The boy?"

"Has been taken care of. All he needs now is to rest. Perhaps you could look in tomorrow?"

"I'm in no hurry." She moved towards the bed, smoothed back the hair from the pale face. "I could sit with him for a while." She added meaningfully, "I'm sure that you have other things to do."

To go downstairs, to find the woman who ran the hotel, to give her money for Leon's keep, more money to be given him when he woke. The cost of a Low passage which he would be a fool to use too soon, but Dumarest couldn't leave him stranded.

There was trouble at the field. Dumarest sensed it as he approached the gate, slowing as he studied the men standing around. Too many men and too many of them without apparent duties. Hard men with blank faces who needed no uniforms to betray their profession. Guards and agents, watchful and alert.

They stood in patches of shadow, scarcely moving, rigid with the patience which was part of their trade. A pair of them stepped forward as a man neared the gate, a tall figure wearing gray, the material scuffed, his feet unsteady.

"You there!" One of the guards shone a flashlight into a flushed and blinking face. "Name?"

"Connors. Why?"

"Just answer. You from the workings?"

"Say, what the hell is this all about?"

"Just answer. Rawf?"

"It could be," said his companion. "He fits the rough description. Mister, you'd better come with us."

"Me? What for? Like hell I will!"

"Suit yourself," said the first man. "You want it hard, you get it hard. Rawf!"

The sap made a flat, dull sound as it landed against the man's temple, knocking him into an unconscious heap.

Thoughtfully Dumarest turned away. The field sealed, a cyber landed—he felt the closing jaws of a trap. Soon the hospitals would be checked, the doctors, it wouldn't take long for Hsi to connect isolated incidents. Connect them and extrapolate and predict exactly where he was to be found. And, on Tradum, places were few in which he could hide. The city, the workings, the areas beyond the mountains impossible to reach on foot. Even the Hyead couldn't live off the land here, between the mountains and the sea. And any attempt to hire transport would leave a trail.

The field—it had to be the field and the first ship to leave. But, already, he had left it too late.

"Man Dumarest!"

The voice came from the shadows, a slight figure in the darkness making a formless blur. One which became a stunted shape, horned, a hand extended for candy.

"Word, man Dumarest. One in scarlet has landed. You promised a high reward."

To a creature at the workings—another proof of the rudimentary telepathic ability Dumarest suspected the Hyead possessed.

"You are late with the word," he said gently. "But the reward will be given. Can you help me more?"

"How, man Dumarest?"

"I want to get on the field unseen. Can it be done?"

"By us, no."

"By others?"

"It is possible. The one known as Kiasong could help. He is to be found—"

"Thank you," said Dumarest. "I know where he is to be found."

Ayantel was closing down when he arrived, saying nothing as he took the heavy shutters from her hands, watching as he set them into position. The interior of the stall was hot, the air scented with spice and roasted meats. A single lamp threw a cone of brilliance over the counter and cooking apparatus, shadows clustering in the corners. Among them the Hyead bustled, cleaning, polishing skewers, setting cooked food to one side, piling the rest into containers of lambent fluid.

"I'm glad you came back," she said when the stall was sealed. "You know my name, what's yours?"

He told her, watching her eyes. If she recognized it she gave no sign.

"Earl," she mused. "Earl Dumarest. I like it, it has a good sound. I'm glad that you didn't lie."

"You would have known?"

"I knew that you were coming." Her hand lifted, gestured at the Hyead. "Kiasong told me. Don't ask me how he knew—sometimes I think they can pick up voices from the wind. He said you needed help. Is that right?"

"Yes. I—"

"Later." Turning she said, "Kiasong, that'll be all for now. Take the cooked food and give half to the monk. You've got the key?"

"Yes, woman Ayantel."

"Then get on your way."

"Wait." Dumarest handed the creature a coin. "For candy—and for silence."

"It is understood, man Dumarest."

"Odd," she said as Kiasong left. "They creep about like ghosts, work for scraps, and yet at times they make me feel like an ignorant savage. Why is that, Earl?"

"A different culture, Ayantel. A different set of values. As far as we are concerned, they have no ambition. They live for the moment—or perhaps they live

in the past. Or, again, they could regard this life as
merely a stepping stone to another."

"Or, maybe they're just practical," she said. "We all
have to die so why fight against the inevitable? Why
wear yourself out trying to get rich when the worms
will win in the end anyway?"

"You're a philosopher."

"No, just a woman who thinks too much at times."

"And generous."

"Because I give Kiasong a few scraps and a place to
sleep? No, I'm practical. The food will go to waste anyway, and with him sleeping in here I've got a cheap
watchman." Shrugging she added, "To hell with that.
Let's talk about you. You need help—trouble?"

"Yes."

"I figured it might be something like that. What did
you do, kill a man?"

"A pilferer called Brad. I don't know his other name
but he had friends."

"Brad." She frowned. "Did you have to kill him?"

"He had a gun. It was him or me."

"A gun? Muld Evron arms his scavengers. Brad,"
she said again. "Medium build, dark hair, scarred
cheek? Operates with a runt called Elvach?" She
thinned her lips at his nod. "One of Evron's boys. You
were smart to pull out. You'd be smarter to get the hell
off this world before they catch up with you. Is that
what you're after?"

Dumarest nodded, letting her make the natural assumption. "I can pay," he said. "If you can fix it I can
pay."

"That helps," she admitted. "But it'll take time. In
the meanwhile you'd better stay out of sight. Got a
place to stay?"

"I can find one."

"And bump into one of Evron's scavengers? No,
Earl, I've go a better idea. You can stay with me." She
stepped towards him, light glinting from her eyes, her
hair. Her flesh held the warm scent of spice, the odor

of femininity. She lifted her arms to his shoulders, aware of the movement of her breasts, the temptation they presented. "You've no objection?"

"No," he said. "I've no objection."

Chapter FIVE

The room was small, warmly intimate, filled with trifles and soft furnishings; a stuffed animal with glassy eyes, a faded bunch of flowers, a box which chimed when opened. The bed was a frilled oasis of hedonistic comfort, the pillows edged with lace, the sheets scented with floral perfumes. A carved idol nodded over a plume of incense, a gilded clock registered the passing hours.

Dumarest stretched, remembering the night, the warm, demanding heat of the woman, the almost savage intensity of her embrace. A thing of need, not affection, though he suspected that affection could come and turn into love. On her side, not his. He could afford no hampering chains.

"Earl, awake yet?"

She came from the bathroom, smiling, radiant. The thin material of the robe she wore did nothing to hide the swell of hips and thighs, the liquid movement of her breasts. She stooped and kissed him, her lips lingering, his own body responding to her proximity. A hunger as pressing as her own, a need as intense.

Later, lying side by side, they talked.

"You're nice," she said. "Gentle. A lot of men think they have to be rough. I guess they reckon they have to prove something, but not you." The tip of her finger traced the scars on his chest. "Knives?"

"Yes."

"In the ring?" She didn't wait for his nod. "A fighter. I guessed as much. You have the look, the walk. Why do men do it, Earl? For kicks? For money?

50

To stand and slash at someone with a naked blade, to get cut in turn, crippled or killed. And for what?"

For the titivation of a jaded crowd, men and women hungry for the sight of blood and pain, revelling in the vicarious danger. Lying back on the scented pillows, Dumarest could see them as he had too often before. A ring of faces, more animal than human, leaning forward from the gilded balconies of arenas, edging the square of a ring, shouting, screaming, filling the air with the scent of feral anticipation.

And, always, there was the fear, the taint mixed with the smell of sweat and oil and blood. The knowledge that a slip, a single error, a momentary delay and death would come carried on a naked blade.

"Why, Earl?" she insisted. "Why did you fight?"

"For money."

"Just that?" Her finger ran over his naked body drifting, caressing. "A man like you could get it in other ways. A rich woman needing a plaything, a man needing a guard. No?"

"No."

"Why not, Earl? You don't want to feed off a woman, right? And to be a guard is to take orders. I don't think you'd like to do that, take orders, I mean. But if you had the chance to be your own boss? To own your own business?"

He said, dryly, "Such as a stall in a market?"

"It's a living."

"For you, maybe. Not for me."

"Not good enough for you?" Her voice hardened a little. "Both the stall and me, perhaps? Is that it, Earl?"

"Is that what you think?"

"Then tell me I'm wrong," she demanded. "Tell me!"

"A stall selling succulent meats," he said bleakly. "Endless food—can you guess what that means to a traveler? I've known men who ate insects in order to stay alive, grass, slime, the droppings of birds. And a woman like yourself—a gift to any man walking under any sun."

"But not you, Earl." Reaching out she rested her fingers on his lips. "Don't argue, I know, you have to keep moving. Traveling, going from world to world, always drifting, never settling down. Why, Earl? What makes you do it?"

He said, "I'm looking for something. A planet called Earth."

"Earth?" He heard her sharp inhalation, the note of incredulity when next she spoke. "You must be joking. No world has that name."

"One does."

"But—Earth?"

"It's an old world," he said, his eyes on the ceiling, the cracks it contained. "The surface is scarred and torn by ancient wars. A great moon hangs in the sky and the stars are few at night. It's a real place, despite what legends say. I know, I was born there."

"And you want to go back?"

"Yes."

"Then why can't you? If you left it, you must know where it lies?"

"I was young," he said. "A scared and hungry boy. I stowed away on a ship and was luckier than I deserved. The captain could have evicted me. Instead, he allowed me to work my passage. I stayed with him until he died, then moved on."

Ship after ship, journey after journey, and each taking him closer to the Center where stars were close and habitable worlds thick. Moving on until even the name of Earth had been forgotten. The coordinates unregistered, unknown.

And then the search, the endless seeming quest, the hunt for clues. Earth existed, he knew it. One day, with luck, he would find it. One day.

"Earl." Her hands were gentle as they touched his forehead, his cheek. The caress a mother would give to a child, soothing, comforting. "Just don't worry about it, darling."

She thought he was deluded, maybe a little disturbed, a man following an empty dream. An impression he was content to leave.

"When will you set about making the arrangements for me to get on the field?"

"Later." She stretched beside him, muscles bunching, rounding the contours of her thighs, accentuating her torso, narrowing her waist. "Earl?"

The idol nodded, smiling as the clock ticked on, murdering the day.

The rendezvous was at dusk down by the wharves, in a small hut which held the stench of rotting fish, brine, the musty odor of nets. Dumarest was cautious as he approached. The woman could be genuine, but her contact have other ideas. Twice he scouted the area and then, satisfied he was not being followed, ducked through the narrow door. Stepping immediately to one side, his eyes were wide as he searched the inner gloom.

"You Dumarest?"

The voice came from one side, a harsh rasp which echoed from the rafters, the roof which half-filled one side of the hut. As Dumarest answered a light flared, settled to a glow. A lantern fed by rancid oil, fuming, adding to the smell. In its light, he could see a tall thin man with narrowed eyes and a mouth pulled upward by a scar into a perpetual sneer.

"Elmar Shem," he said. "We have a mutual friend, right?"

"Maybe."

"You're careful, I like that. Well, mister, if the price is right we can do business. What do you offer me to get on the field?"

"Unseen?"

"That's the deal. How much?"

"Fifty."

"Too bad, mister, someone's been wasting my time."

"And another fifty when we part." Dumarest stepped forward towards the lamp, the table on which it stood. "A hundred total. Easy money for little work."

Shem sucked in his breath. He wore a faded uniform with tarnished braid. A checker at the field who owed the woman a favor and, so she'd claimed, could be trusted. Dumarest wasn't so sure.

"Well?"

"It's low," Shem complained. "They've got the field sewed up real tight. Every man is scrutinized and every load searched. God knows what they want you for, but it has to be something big."

"Me? Are they looking for me?"

"You fit the description." Shem hesitated. "There's even talk of a reward for the man who turns you in."

"From whom? Evron?"

"Well—"

"You're lying," snapped Dumarest. "And even if you're not, it's none of my concern. Evron's after me. He could be watching the gate and I don't want to be shot in the back as I pass through. Now, do we make a deal or not?"

"A hundred?"

"That's what I said."

"Then that's what it'll have to be." Shem produced a bottle, poured, handed Dumarest a glass. "Drink to seal the bargain?"

Dumarest lifted the glass, pressed it to his closed lips, watching Shem's eyes. They lifted, flickered, fell again.

"How many ships are on the field?"

"Five—you want specifications?"

"No. Are more expected soon?"

"Two should arrive at dawn, another three before nightfall. We're pretty busy at the moment."

Good news, if ships were due to arrive then others must be ready to leave. Cargo vessels ferrying processed metals, others with loads of contract-workers, still more with imported staples. The workings made a ceaseless demand on men and machine replacements, explosives and tools—all which had to be fetched in from nearby worlds.

Dumarest said, "How are you going to work it?"

"I'm in charge of a bunch of workers. I'll get you a set of dungarees, you change, join the bunch and walk in with us. I can vouch for you, and arrange for a man to fall out so you can replace him. It won't be easy, but if we pick the right time it can be managed. I'll need the advance now."

Dumarest said, casually, "I've seen the gate. They check each man individually. How are you going to get over that?"

"I told you, they trust me. Hell, man, you want me to help you or not?"

"I'll think about it. See you here this time tomorrow?"

"Hell, no!" Shem lifted his voice. "Evron!"

Dumarest smashed aside the lamp. It fell on a mass of wadded nets, bursting, sending tongues of flame over the oiled strands. A thread of gun fire spat from the roofed section, the report of the pistol muffled, a vicious cough, splinters flying as lead slammed into the table. Shem cried out, falling backwards, the victim of bad aiming. Dumarest crouched, his shoulder against a wall, the pale frame of the door to one side. From the burnings nets rose a thick cloud of rancid smoke.

"Muld! The fire! We'll be burned alive!"

"Shut up, watch the door, shoot if he tries to escape." The voice was a feral purr. "Crell, Van, you drop from the back and go around the sides. Move!"

A trap, baited and primed. Only his instinctive caution had saved him from the closing jaws. But he still had to get out.

Dumarest tensed, pressed against the wooden planks at his side, felt something yield a little. Reaching out he found something hard and round, a float for one of the nets. He threw it to the far side of the hut, rising as it left his hand, throwing his full weight against the planking as it fell.

Wood splintered, nails yielding with a harsh squeal, smoke following him through the opening as he lunged outside. Something tore at his scalp to send blood over

his cheek, and a giant's hammer slammed at his left
heel.

Then he was out, running, dodging as a figure rose
before him, one arm lifted, aiming, the hand heavy
with the weight of a gun.

A hand which fell beneath the upward slash of his
knife, the figure staggering, screaming, trying to quench
the fountain of blood gushing from the stump of his
wrist.

Dumarest stooped, snatched up the discarded
weapon, tore the severed hand from the butt and, lifting it, closed his finger on the trigger. Three shots
aimed low and in a tight fan. Three bullets a little
higher, the second echoed by a shriek, the sound of a
falling body.

Evron's snarling voice. "Back, you fools, he's
armed!"

Dumarest turned. The man with the severed hand
was leaning against a bollard, his face ghastly in the
thickening dust, a crimson pool at his feet. Beyond him
men came running, fishermen intent on saving their nets,
boathooks and gaffs held in their hands. A near-mob
who would not be gentle. Past the hut, leading to a
ridge and a road, ran a narrow path.

Dumarest raced towards it, almost fell, regained his
balance as bullets hit the dirt inches from his feet.
Quickly he emptied the gun at the burning hut, threw it
aside and headed for the road. A ditch lay on the other
side and he ducked into it, crouching low, a blur
among the vegetation which almost filled the narrow
gully.

From above came the sound of running feet and
panting breath.

"A set up," the voice was bitter. "Crell dead and
Van without a hand. Shem—"

"To hell with Shem!" The feral purr was savage.
"He should have handled it different, instead he must
have aroused suspicion. Get the raft. He's got to be
around here somewhere. We'll lift and drift. Move!"

"Why bother?" The third voice was cynical. "He'll

go back to the woman. All we have to do is to get there first and wait."

"The woman." Evron chuckled. "Sure, why didn't I think of that? Good thinking, Latush. We'll meet with her and have a party."

Three of them, close, lost in anticipation of lust and bestiality. Within minutes they would be airborne and out of reach. Dumarest could wait until they had gone, make his own way to the field and do his best to elude the watchers.

But the woman had been kind. He rose, moving silently, a shadow among other shadows, seeing the three silhouettes dim against the sky. Two facing each other, a third moving away down the road, obviously to collect the raft. His hand dipped, rose, lifted with the knife, moved forward to send the steel slamming into the exposed back. As the man fell he sprang up onto the road and lunged forward, hands stiffened, blunt axes which lifted and fell.

Latush died first, his neck broken as he turned, eyes glazed as he fell. Evron was luckier. With the instinct of a rat he dodged, one hand clawing at his belt, mouth opening to shout or plead.

Dumarest hit him, bone snapping beneath his hand, the reaching hand falling from the belt. He struck again and blood spouted from the pulped nose.

"For God's sake!" Evron backed, his broken arm swinging, the other lifted in mute appeal. "You can't kill me, man! You can't!"

"A party," said Dumarest thickly. "Enjoy it you swine—in hell!"

He stabbed, the tips of his fingers crushing the larnyx then, as Evron doubled, chopped at the base of the neck.

Like a crushed toad the man slumped, dying, vomiting blood.

"Hey!" A voice called from beside the smouldering hut. "There's a dead man here. God, look at the blood!"

"Here's another, shot. What's been going on?"

Murder, violence and sudden death. Execution dealt to those who deserved it. A threat eliminated and something gained. Money and a raft, the wealth they carried on them, the vehicle parked nearby. Dumarest could use both.

"Earl!" Ayantel stared from her open door, her eyes shocked. "God, man, you look like hell!"

Blood which had dried in ugly smears, dirt and slime on his clothing and boots, his hands begrimed, his hair a mess. He could have washed in the sea, but it would have risked too much. Instead he had flown high in the raft, looking, waiting, dropping down to the roof of her apartment, lashing the raft firmly before climbing down to a window, then her landing.

He said, quickly, "Let me in."

"You hurt?" Her voice was tense as she closed the door after him.

"No, but I could use a bath."

"A bath and a drink, by the look of it. What happened?" Her lips tensed as he answered. "Shem, the bastard! He sold you out. Me too. Earl, if Evron—"

"He won't."

"But—"

"Evron is dead. I dumped him and two of his boys into the sea." Dumarest dropped the bag he had carried slung around his neck by a belt. "You don't have to worry about him, Ayantel. Not now, or ever again. Now, where's that drink?"

It was good and he relished it, before stepping fully dressed under the shower, rubbing the dirt and blood from his clothing, the mess from his boots. Stripping, he bathed as the woman dried his gear. Aside from the lacerations on his scalp, he was unharmed. The bullet which had hit his boot had done no more than tear the heel.

Clean, drying himself on a fluffy towel, he rejoined the woman, pouring himself another drink.

"So Shem set you up," she said. "I'm sorry, Earl. I thought I could trust him."

"Am I blaming you?"

"No, but you have the right." She poised the knife, remembering the traces of blood it had carried, the smears. "How many?"

"Does it matter?"

"I want to know, Earl." Her hand tightened around the hilt as he told her what had happened. "You were lucky," she said. "No, clever. You guessed that they would be waiting. What tipped you off?"

"Shem offered me a drink, but he didn't join me. The stuff was drugged. And he couldn't keep his eyes from the roof. When I questioned him he had the wrong answers. As for the rest, forget it, it's over."

"Easy to say," she said, "not easy to do. You could have been killed. A wasted night, all for nothing."

"No," he corrected. "Not for nothing."

The bag lay where he had dropped it. Opened, it revealed wallets, rings, heavy-banded chronometers—the loot he had collected from the dead. Quickly he sorted it. Evron, as most of his breed, had liked to carry a fat roll. His aides had emulated him.

"This is for you." He handed a wad of cash to the woman. "I'll take the jewelery—you don't want to risk having it traced."

"No." She shook her head as she stared at the money. "No, Earl, I haven't earned it. I don't deserve it."

"Wrong on both counts," he said curtly. "You have and you will. Can you fly a raft?"

"Yes. Why?"

"I've got one on the roof. Now listen, this is what I want you to do."

She frowned as he explained. "Now?"

"Now." Before the alarm could be given, the authorities begin to investigate. And before the cyber, sitting like a gaunt red spider in his web, could learn new facts with which to build a prediction to gain him high rewards, and the Cyclan could get what they wanted most of all.

The secret which had been stolen from one of their

hidden laboratories. The correct sequence in which the fifteen molecular units needed to be joined, in order to create the affinity twin.

Kalin had passed it on to him, the girl with the flame-red hair Earl would never forget. Brasque had stolen it, destroying the records, dying in turn to keep it safe. Fifteen biological molecular units, the last reversed to determine dominant or submissive characteristics.

An artificial symbiote which, when injected into the bloodstream, nestled at the base of the cortex and took control of the entire nervous and sensory systems. The brain containing the dominant half would take over the body of the host. Literally take over. Each move, every touch, all sound and sight and taste, all would be transmitted. In effect, it gave an old man the power to become young again in a new, virile body. A body he would keep until it was destroyed, or his own died.

It would give the Cyclan the galaxy to use as a plaything.

The mind of a cyber would reside in each and every ruler and person of consequence. They would be helpless marionettes moving to the dictates of their masters. Slaves of the designs of those who wore the scarlet robes.

They knew of the secret and would discover it in time. But too much time, the possible combinations ran into millions, was needed to test them all. Even at the rate of one every second, it would take four thousand years.

Dumarest could cut that time down to a handful of hours. Once they had him they could probe his brain, learn what they needed to know, advance their domination like a red stain spread on the stars.

"Earl?"

He blinked, conscious that he had fallen into a reverie, hovered on the brink of sleep. Standing, he looked at the woman. She wore a casual gown, a flower in her hair, too much paint on her face. The scent of her perfume was overpowering.

"Is this what you wanted, Earl?"

"Yes." He gripped her shoulders and stared into her eyes. "Make no mistake, girl. My life is in your hands now. You know what to do?"

"I know."

"Good." He turned, picked up the bottle of brandy, spilled the contents over her hair, her shoulders, her gown. "Then let's go."

Chapter SIX

It was late and Dach Lang was tired. For five hours he had stood guard at the gate. Now it was his turn to make a patrol around the inner perimeter of the fence. A long journey and a useless one. The summit was fitted with alarms. If anyone tried to climb the mesh, they would be shocked and caught. Yet the orders had been plain.

"Dach!" The figure approaching was muffled, his face shadowed by the peak of his cap, his collar turned high. Haw Falla felt the chill. "A bad night," he grumbled. "And still hours to wait before dawn. This kind of thing makes a man wish for his bed."

"You're late."

"I had things to do." Falla shrugged aside the accusation. "A man has his needs."

Too many and too often as far as Falla was concerned, but that was his problem. Dach checked his watch, made a notation on his pad and tucked the book away. Three minutes late. With luck they could make it up, but in any case he was in the clear. Two-man patrols, the orders had said, and a two-man patrol it would be.

"Let's get on our way."

It was growing cold, the wind from the sea carrying a drift of rain, sparkles clinging to the mesh of the fence, glittering like minute gems beneath the glow of the floodlights. An artistic scene, but one which neither man appreciated. They kept their eyes down, searching for holes, for strangers.

Not that it was easy. The ships stood close, crewmen busy, making a straggling line from their vessels to the

gate. Accustomed to the freedom of space they resented
the new restrictions, the checks and questions at the
gate. There had been a little trouble, a couple of fights,
some broken heads.

Well, to hell with them. Dach had his own problems.
He brooded on them as Falla led the way around the
perimeter. Sulen was fully grown now and getting reb-
ellious. Mari didn't help, what with her spendthrift
ways. A woman should look after her daughter, take a
closer interest in what she was getting in to. Instead,
she spend hard-earned money on clothes and paint
which made her look like a creature from a seraglio. A
shame and a disgrace to any decent, hard-working
man. And the chances were high that if he went home
now, she would be out or not alone.

"Dach!" Falla halted, staring up at the sky. "What
the hell—look, a raft!"

It swept down low, almost touching the summit of
the fence, veering over the field as alarms sounded
from the gate. From it came the sound of singing,
high-pitched laughter, the trill of a woman's voice.

"The stupid bitch!" Falla began to run, waving his
arms. "Hey, you up there! You crazy or something?"

Insane or drunk, the only reasonable explanation.
No one flew over a field, the risk was too great. With
ships leaving and landing at any time, the air-displace-
ment would wreck any smaller craft. A fact Dumarest
had known, a risk he had taken.

He lay flat in the body of the raft, invisible from below, tensing as the vehicle jerked beneath Ayantel's
inexperienced hands. She was acting well, a little too
well. Only by a tremendous effort did she avoid being
thrown over the edge.

"Careful!"

"I can manage," she whispered. Then, loudly, "Hey,
down there! You wanna drink? You wanna join the
party? Hows about us all getting together?"

"Mad," said Dach. "Stinking drunk and crazy.
Watch out!"

He ducked as the raft swept over his head, dropped

to vanish behind a ship, lifted again immediately to swing towards them, to smack against the ground.

"Whew!" Ayantel fanned herself, then reached for a bottle. "That was rough. Here, friends, help yourself!"

A spoiled bitch, the product of decadent luxury, half-naked, stinking of liquor, out on a crazy spree. Yet she had to be rich, or have wealthy friends. Rafts were expensive on Tradum, especially the small, personal-carrier kind.

Dach slowed as Falla gripped his arm.

"Take it easy, now. Handle her gently."

"She should be canned!"

"Sure, but what'll it get you?" Gifted with the survival cunning of an animal Falla moved closer to the raft, the woman it contained. "Now, madam," he said soothingly, "you shouldn't be here. I'll have to take care of you. If you'll just step out of that raft—"

"Go to hell!"

"It's for you own protection. I'll call your friends and have them take you home. You don't want to risk your pretty neck in a place like this."

"Here!" Falla dodged as a bottle swept towards his head. As it landed with a shatter of breaking glass, the raft lifted. "So long, boys—buy yourselves a drink!"

Money fluttered down, a shower of notes, landing as the raft lifted over the fence. Too high to be stopped, and to shoot it down was to invite later trouble.

"Falla, she's—"

"Get the money, man!" Falla was practical. "We can't stop her now."

No one could stop her. Within minutes she would land, change, vanish into the night. The harlot had appeared unrecognizable as the woman who sold meats at a stall.

Dumarest rose from where he had jumped, keeping the bulk of a ship between himself and the guards. The loading port was open, a handler staring interestedly at the couple chasing the scattered wealth.

"When you leaving?"

"What?" He turned, looking at Dumarest. "Not until noon."

"Anything due earlier?"

"The *Hamanara,* she's loaded and set. And there's the *Golquin* over to your right. Say, did you see that dame in the raft?"

"A looker."

"You can say that again." The handler sighed, enviously. "Rich too. See how she scattered that loot? Hell, some men have all the luck. You looking for a passage?"

"That or a berth."

"Try the *Golquin*. Their steward had an argument at the gate and got his head broken. You could be lucky."

It was a vessel which had seen better days. The plates were stained, scarred, patches breaking the smooth lines of the original design. The ramp was worn, the lights dim beyond the open port, the air filled with a musty taint due to ancient filters and bad circulation. The captain matched his ship.

He stood glowering in the passage leading into the heart of the vessel, a squat man with suspicious eyes, heavy brows which joined to form a russet bar, a short beard which hid a trap of a mouth.

"A berth?"

"If you have one, Captain, yes." Dumarest added, casually, "I heard that your steward ran into some trouble."

"He was drunk and a fool. You've handled the job before?"

"Yes."

"If you're lying you'll regret it." Captain Shwarb rocked back on his heels, thinking. "The gate," he said. "Did you have trouble coming through?"

"None—what's it all about anyway?"

"Damned if I know or care. Can you operate a table?" Shwarb grunted at Dumarest's nod. "Good. Well, this is the deal. No pay, hard work and a half of what you win is mine. Take it or leave it."

A hard bargain, but Dumarest was in no position to argue. "I'll take it, Captain. When do we leave?"

"In thirty minutes. You bunk with Arishall. We're bound for Mailarette." He added, grimly, "A warning. You look straight, but you could be kinked. If I catch you using analogues you go outside. Understand?"

Arishall was the engineer, one of fading skill and advancing years. A quiet man with mottled skin and pale blue eyes. He rose from his bunk as Dumarest entered the cabin and introduced himself.

"The new steward, eh?" Arishall waved to a cabinet. "That's yours. Urian's about your size so his gear should fit. Want some advice?"

"Such as?"

"Stay off kicks. The captain—"

"I know. He told me."

"Don't think he doesn't mean it. He lost his wife to a guy who thought he was a gorilla. Since then he can't stand anyone who uses analogs. I can't say that I blame him. A man's a man, why the hell he should want to adopt the characteristics of a beast I can't imagine. You drink?"

"At times."

"With me it's medicine." Arishall produced a bottle and drank from its neck. "This is between us, right?"

Dumarest nodded, opening the cabinet and taking out the uniform it contained. It was clean, the colors bright, and stripping he donned it. A box held a hypogun and a container of drugs, quicktime and the neutralizer. Checking the instrument, Dumarest loaded it with ampuls from the container.

"How many crew?"

"Me, Shwarb, Dinok the navigator."

"No handler?"

"I double up and you help me if I need it." The engineer drank from the bottle again. "The *Golquin's* a free trader—or didn't you know?"

The condition of the vessel had told him that, the minimum crew made it obvious. Operating on a low budget, making a profit where and how it could, the crew paid by shares after all expenses had been covered. Some free traders were better than others—the *Golquin* was one of the worst.

"Yes," said Dumarest. "I knew."

"And you don't care?"

"Working a passage is better than paying."

"And you've worked on free traders before, right?" Arishall pursed his lips as Dumarest nodded. "Good. It helps. Do a good job and maybe Shwarb will offer you a regular berth. He's hard, but fair." He took a final drink. "Well, I'd better get with it. See you, Earl."

The alarm sounded twenty minutes later. Dumarest made the seal-check and reported to the control room. Two minutes later he felt the vibration of the drive, the lift of the vessel as the Erhaft field was established, carrying the ship up and out towards the stars. A man-made missile moving at a velocity against which that of light was a crawl.

Taking the hypogun, he went into the salon. Five passengers were riding High; a grizzled mining engineer, a suave entrepreneur, a trader and two women, neither of them young, both of them retiring from the stress of an ancient profession before they hit the bottom. One smiled as he approached.

"This is a bonus. A steward who looks like a man. Can you give a girl relaxation if she can't sleep, mister?"

"Cut it out, Hilma," said her companion tiredly. "If you hope to pick up a husband on Mailarette you'd better learn to watch your tongue."

"Old habits, Chi." The woman shrugged. "But I guess you're right. Well, friend, where do you want to put it?"

"In the neck."

Dumarest lifted the hypogun as the woman tilted her head, firing the charge of drug into her bloodstream. The reaction was immediate. She seemed to freeze, to become a statue as her metabolism slowed. Each act, the blink of an eye, a breath, the lift of a finger took forty times longer than normal.

Within seconds the other passengers had been treated. As Dumarest turned from the last, he saw a man standing and watching from the door of the salon.

"So you're Dumarest," he said. "I'm Dinok, the navigator."

His uniform was impeccable, the material carrying the sheen of newness, braid and insignia gleaming with polish. A small man, fastidious in his appearance, Dinok wore his hair short, his face hairless aside from a thin moustache. His hands were smooth, the nails polished, neatly filed.

"Neat," he approved, glancing at the passengers. "You hit them where it counted. I like to see a man who knows his work."

"Did Shwarb send you to check?"

"Would you care if he did?" Dinok shrugged, not waiting for an answer. "Now you clean the cabins, prepare the basic, fill the hoppers and then get to work at the table." He glanced at where cards and dice stood on an expanse of green baize. "If it's your style to cheat, don't get caught."

Dumarest lifted the hypogun. "When do you want it?"

"The captain and me take care of ourselves. Give Arishall a shot after you've done the chores—but I guess you know the system." Dinok pursed his lips as he stared at the women, the men. "Scum," he said. "But the best we can hope for. If you get tips you'll be lucky."

Dumarest caught the note of disdain in the man's voice and could guess the reason. Dinok had been used to better things. An officer, perhaps, on a luxury vessel where a part of his duty would have been to entertain. A good job for a man with the inclination to do it— one he would have hated to lose.

He said, casually, "When did they book?"

"We got them from the agent, some could have been waiting for weeks. But you? What made you join the *Golquin?*"

"I needed the job."

"Don't we all?" Dinok scowled, a man caught in a trap of his own making. Drink or drugs, or an alliance with the wrong woman at the wrong time. Something had sent him on the downward path which, as yet, hadn't ended. That would come when he grew careless about his appearance, casual as to his duties. Then, he would be kicked out to rot on some lonely world. "Well, Earl, I'll leave you to it. Watch out for the entrepreneur—I don't trust his type."

Ren Dhal was smooth, skilled, deft with the dice and clever with the cards. A man who had established a small business on Tradum, selling out when the opposition grew too strong. Moving on now to seek fresh opportunities.

"They're everywhere," he said as he sat at the table. "But it takes a smart brain to recognize them. On Heiglet, for example, I noticed that three taverns were competing. I arranged a merger, raised the prices and took a nice profit. All it required was some fast talking."

Dumarest dealt the cards, playing without real interest, merely doing a part of his job. As always on any journey, life had settled into a routine. Play and talk passed the time. Work a little more when, the quicktime in his blood neutralized, he attended to what had to be done.

The cabins searched, baggage checked, looking for any signs that the passengers were not exactly what they claimed to be. He had found nothing suspicious.

"Time to eat," he announced, and went to draw the rations of basic. Elementary food, a liquid thick with protein, sickly with glucose, laced with vitamins and essential elements. A cup would provide enough energy for a day.

The trader grunted as he accepted his ration. A dour man who spent long hours studying lists of figures, computing his margins of profit. He rarely spoke and seemed to hold a grievance against the grizzled engineer who had formed an attachment with one of the women, careless as to her past.

"Food." Chi pulled a face. "Is that what you call it? Hilma, we could be making a mistake. On Tradum, at least we had something decent to eat."

"And will again." Hilma glanced at the engineer. He was old, but he had money and was as good as she could hope to get. Smiling she said, "To the future, Gramon, may it be pleasant."

"I'll drink to that." He sipped, beaming. "It'll be good to settle down. I've had enough of traveling and I've breathed in all the rock dust my lungs will take. Say, Chi, I've a friend who might be interested in you. A farmer—you got objections to living on a farm?"

The nearest thing to hell she could imagine, but a man could be changed and, if he owned land, he was worth looking at.

"His own farm?"

"Of course. Warsh and me grew up together. His wife died a decade ago and I figure it's time he got another. Tell you what, I'll fix it up as soon as we land. Have dinner together and talk things over. Agreed?"

They were talking too much, ignoring the table, and Dumarest riffled the cards.

"What'll it be, friends? Starsmash, olkay, nine-nap, spectrum?" They weren't interested, not that it mattered. Dumarest could take Shwarb's disappointment. And, soon now, the journey would be over.

They landed at dawn, when the terminator was bisecting the field, early mist blurring outlines, a thin fog which had not yet burned away. Dumarest stood at the head of the ramp as was expected. Dinok had been right, there were no tips.

"With a bunch like that you're lucky to get a smile," scowled Arishall. "How did you make out at the table?"

"Poor."

"Bad news for the captain." Arishall shrugged. "Well, he can't grumble. In this game you have to take it as it comes. Earl, I need your help."

Dumarest glanced at the field, the mist. It was a good time to leave.

"It won't take long," said the engineer. "A dump-job down in the hold. Some poor devil didn't make it."

He looked very small as he lay in the casket designed for the transportation of beasts, but in which men could ride, doped, frozen and ninety-percent dead. Riding Low, risking the fifteen-percent death rate for the sake of cheap travel. A gamble which he had taken once too often.

"A kid," said Arishall. "I didn't want to take him, but Shwarb insisted."

Dumarest made no comment, looking at the ceiling where someone with a touch of imagination had painted a smiling face. A woman's face with liquid eyes and a softly inviting mouth, hair which was wreathed in a mass of golden curls over a smooth brow. Her throat accentuated the slope of the shoulders, the upper curves of barely portrayed breasts which vanished into a depicted cloud, a mass of vapor which framed the portrait with a milky fleece. The last thing Leon Harvey had seen.

"A kid," said Arishall again. "I guessed he wouldn't make it. He was too thin, too puny. He should have waited, fattened himself up—well, to hell with it. It's all a part of the job."

"Something wrong?" Dinok entered the hold and frowned as he looked at the dead boy. "Hell, I know him."

"From where?" Dumarest was sharp. "Nerth?"

"Nerth? No, Shajok. It was his first trip."

"Are you sure about that?"

Dinok shrugged. "I'd gamble on it, Earl. You know how it is with first-timers. No matter how they try to cover it up, it shows. The kid was green. He didn't know enough to argue about the price when Shwarb cheated him. He was in a sweat, eager to get away. Knowing Shajok, I can't blame him."

"Arishall?"

"I remember Shajok, but not the boy," said the engineer. "Urian handled it. I was busy getting a replacement part for the engine. They had him sealed by the time I got back."

"And when he left?"

"Arishall wouldn't remember that, Earl," said the navigator dryly. "He'd taken a little too much of his medicine. We first dropped the boy on Aestellia and he must have moved on to Tradum. I guess he recognized the *Golquin* and felt at home. Now he's dead. A pity, but that's the way it goes." He stooped, felt under the casket, rose holding the cheap fabric bag Leon had carried in his hand. "Let's see if he left anything worth having."

His clothes, a cheap ring with a chipped stone, a folding knife with a worn blade, a rasp, a thin book, something wrapped in a cloth, a few coins.

Dinok set them aside as he unwrapped the bundle. It contained a slab of gray material six inches long, four wide, three thick; a block of artificial stone which had been roughly carved into the shape of an idol.

"Rubbish." Dinok wasn't disappointed, those who traveled Low carried little else. "A hobby, I guess. It looks as if he'd worked on it. Want it, Arishall?"

"No, nor this junk either." The engineer tossed aside the book. "It's all yours if you want it, Earl. You take the gear and we'll split the coins. A deal?"

"I can use the bag." Dumarest lifted it, filled it with the idol, the book and other items. "I'll dump the rest."

"Talking about dumping, we'd better get on with the job. You'd better lift him, Earl, while I—"

"I've quit," said Dumarest. "Dinok can give you a hand."

The mist was slow in clearing. While it held, traffic would be scanty. A café beyond the gate sold a variety of cheap food and drink. Dumarest bought a mug of coffee and sat nursing it, looking at the few others the establishment contained. It was early yet. Later it would fill with workers, transients, crews assembling and killing a little time, agents on the look-out for cheap labor. All potential sources of information. Now there was time for thought.

Leon was dead and his knowledge had died with him. He must have awoken back at the hotel, finding himself alone, rejected, searching town and field for the man he had believed to be a friend, finding the familiar vessel and booking the only passage he could afford.

A boy who had lied as to the planet of his origin. Shajok, not Nerth, and yet under the primitive truth drug he had stuck to that name.

The name—so tantalizingly similar. And the creed of the Original People, that strange cult which believed in a common world of origin for all the diverse races of mankind. A hidden, secret group who sought no converts but who could, perhaps, hold information of value.

Two scraps of succulent bait for anyone setting a trap—and Dumarest had sensed a trap. But the boy was dead and, by his death, he had proved his innocence.

Dumarest sipped at his coffee and then examined the items he had taken. The clothing was exactly what it appeared to be, cheap materials, the seams welded, unbroken. He ran fingers over every inch, finding nothing hidden there. The ring was a tawdry adornment, probably bought to use as a primitive knuckleduster. Dumarest held it up to the light, turning it as he examined the stone, the interior of the band. Holding the metal he struck the stone forcefully against the surface of the table, checking it as it vibrated from the impact. Nothing.

The worn knife, the rasp and bag were what they appeared to be. The block of artificial stone from which the idol was carved was dense, the surface yielding reluctantly to the touch of the rasp. Dumarest examined it, found the surface uncracked, the mass obviously solid. Setting it down, he picked up the book.

It was a thin publication with plastic covers, the pages crammed with a mass of condensed information. A variety of facts and figures, mathematical formulae, chemical compounds, astronomical data, the coordinates of a thousand worlds, a list of survival techniques to be followed in hostile environments. A book which would be the pride of any adventurous youngster. A thing which a new traveler might think of as essential.

Dumarest flexed the covers, narrowed his eyes as he felt an inconsistency. He lifted the knife from his boot and carefully slid the razor-sharp edge along the interior binding. The point slipped into a narrow opening, lifted it to reveal what had been tucked into the pocket thus made.

A photograph. One showing a smiling woman with a strongly boned face, deep-set eyes of a peculiar amber, pale blonde hair drawn back from her face and held with a metal fillet. Her garb was masculine, pants and tunic of dull green. An elder sister, perhaps, or a relative of some kind. But it wasn't the woman who held Dumarest's interest.

She had been shown standing before a wall topped with a peaked roof, a house or repository of some kind. On it, visible against the dull stone, rested a peculiar design.

Dumarest stared at it, narrowing his eyes, following the lines which joined nodules of brightness, as if fragments of broken glass had been joined and incorporated into a symbolic representation.

A fish. Bright points glinting by reflected light, so that the design gained an added impact.

The fish with shining scales!

Dumarest lowered the photograph, leaning back, barely conscious of the increased activity within the café. A coincidence, it had to be, one more to set beside the rest—and yet coincidences happened. Leon could have belonged to the Original People—that strange, hidden, quasi-religious cult. They could know of the exact whereabouts of Earth. The design could be a visual part of a mnemonic which had once been told to him on a distant world.

The Ram, the Bull, the Heavenly Twins, and next the Crab, the Lion, the Virgin, and the Scales. The

Scorpion, the Archer, the Goat, the Water Bearer, and the Fish with shining scales.

The signs of the zodiac. Twelve symbols, each representing a portion of the sky running in a complete circle. Once he found a world surrounded by those signs, he would have found Earth.

A stellar analogue could do it, patterns set up by a computer, constellations arranged as seen from any viewpoint. Once he could feed in the patterns of stars comprising the zodiac the thing would be done, the long search over.

But first he needed to know just what those stars were, their numbers and disposition. Leon's people could provide the answer. And Leon had come from Shajok.

Chapter SEVEN

It was going to be a good day. Bhol Kinabalu felt it the moment he woke, the feeling reenforced as he drew back the curtains and looked through the window. The wind was brisk from the plains, the pennons set on poles above each house standing steady as they pointed towards the mountains. Opening the window he sniffed at the air, crisp, clean, carrying the scent of ulumen. The harvest promised to be exceptional this year; with only a modicum of luck he would treble his investment.

"My lord." His cheerfulness was contagious. The girl in the bed smiled as she stretched, then sat upright, the covers falling from her naked torso. "Did I find pleasure in your eyes?"

A slight thing, young, yet with a feral determination to survive. Kinabalu could appreciate that as he could appreciate other things; his house, his fortune, the enterprises in which he was involved. He turned from the window, a thick-set, stocky man, his ebon skin glowing with good health. A Hausi, caste marks livid on his cheeks.

"You slept well?"

"Deeply, my lord." Her arms lifted in invitation, falling as, smiling, he shook his head. "No?"

"No." He saw the sudden fear in her eyes and quickly eased her fears. "You please me, girl, but the sun has risen and there is much to do. Hurry now and prepare breakfast. Vinia will tell you what to do."

Vinia who would undoubtedly be jealous, but who was mature enough to recognize that a man needed novelty in his sensuous pursuits. She would train the girl, teach her that there was a time for indulgence, others for food and rest. Demarkations of the day which left the greater proportion of it to the affairs of business.

Business—the very stuff of life to all who belonged to the Hausi.

The meal was simple, tisane, bread toasted and drenched in butter, a portion of sweet compote, a handful of dried fruits. Kinabalu ate slowly, enjoying the tastes and consistency, sipping at the pungent tisane. A good time in which to recall the pleasures of the night, the things needed to be done during the day.

The harvest—it would do no harm to send a man to examine the crop. The farmers were basically honest, yet there always was the temptation to cheat. A little theft was to be expected, but a man sent to check and investigate would keep it to a minimum. Kinabalu made a note and turned to the next item.

The shipment of tools from Elg would arrive today on the *Zandel*. As agent, he must arrange for their transportation to the Shagrib Peninsular. Mayna Chow would arrange it, but there would be haggling over the cost. Mar Zelm at the warehouse was a little too generous in his pricing of the things brought in for trade. Della Ogez was late in her payment. True, trade had been poor, but such delay must not be encouraged. The tavern at the end of Quendel Street—Kinabalu sighed as a knock heralded the entry of Vinia.

"What is it?"

"An urgent call from Jalch Moore, my lord. He insists that you speak with him."

"You should have told him that I was out."

"I apologize, my lord, but—"

"Never mind."

Kinabalu rose from the table, conscious of a flaw in the day. Vinia had done it deliberately, of course, a minor revenge for his having brought another woman into the house. A mistake, perhaps, but one now made and to be lived with. As Jalch Moore had to be lived with—but why was the man so persistent?

He glared from the screen, a thin face with deep-set

eyes, hair the color of sun-bleached straw, a thin mouth, a chin which sported a tuft of beard.

"Kinabalu!" His voice was an angry rasp. "I've been trying to contact you. Where have you been?"

"Busy, my lord."

"On my affairs, I hope. How much longer must I wait?"

Kinabalu masked his irritation. The man was a pest, but his money was good. An agreement made had to be kept.

He said, quietly, "My lord, we have been over this before. The equipment is ready and waiting, but it would be most unwise of you to leave without protection."

"We have arms."

"True, but there are other considerations. You need a guide and a guard, one at least. I have suggested many men who are capable."

"Fools," snapped Moore. "I can read a man as well as most. All you've sent me are idiots who will be more trouble than they are worth. Surely you can find a man of the type I need? Or are you telling me that, on all Shajok, there are nothing but spineless characters hoping for free food and easy pay?"

The man was being unfair and must know it, yet Kinabalu had to admit that he had a point. But what man in his right mind would agree to join such a crazy expedition? They knew of the dangers if Moore did not. A thing he had already explained a dozen times, to no avail.

"The Hausi have a reputation," said Moore bitterly. "I placed all arrangements in your hands with the promise that I would receive satisfaction. I do not think your guild would be happy to learn of my disappointment."

A threat, a minor one, but a threat all the same. The guild would not take kindly to any complaint of such a nature. The failure of one reflected on the abilities of all. Even though Shajok was a relatively unimportant world, any complaint would create an unpleasant situation.

Kinabalu said, soothingly, "My lord, be assured that I am doing my best. I personally guarantee that you will be able to leave very soon now."

"Soon? Just what the hell does that mean?"

"Soon, my lord."

"A day?" Moore was insistent. "Two? Give me a time, man. I have to know."

"Two."

A gamble, but one which had to be taken. Two days to find the right kind of man, one who would satisfy Jalch Moore. If necessary he would offer a bonus—a lost profit, but a maintained reputation. But it need not come to that. The *Zandel* was due in at noon.

It was a small ship operating a regular route, embracing a handful of worlds. Small cargoes and few passengers, but it contacted Vonstate where other ships landed. Aside from occasional free traders, it and one other were the only vessels touching Shajok.

Kinabalu was at the field when it landed, hearing the crack of displaced air from above, watching as it settled in a haze of blue luminescence from its Erhaft field. From force of habit he studied the others waiting. Wen Larz eager for tourists, Zorya hovering in the hope of making a private deal with the crew for anything they may have carried, Frend who needed cheap labor for his mine, Chaque who had nothing better to do.

He nodded to Kinabalu. "How's the new acquisition making out, Bhol?"

An indiscreet question and one in the worst possible taste. The Hausi ignored it.

"Why are you here, Agus?"

"Looking." The man turned towards the vessel, the opening port. "Have you managed to satisfy Moore yet?"

He knew too much, his questions were too pointed, but that was to be expected. A dilettante with time to kill and curiosity to be satisfied. Kinabalu looked at him, studying his roached hair, the face which seemed to be prematurely old, the lines too deep for the youthful skin and eyes.

"I'm working on it."

"And with success?" Chaque parted his lips in silent laughter as the other made no comment. "You'll have to work harder, my friend. Sirey has taken a job with a harvester. I thought that you would like to know."

The guide! Kinabalu thinned his lips. The man had promised, but had obviously broken his word. That, or he had been bribed away. Two men to find now instead of one—and guides were scarce.

"Of course," said Chaque casually, "a replacement could always be found if the price was right. The price or the prospect of satisfaction."

"You?"

"Perhaps."

"What do you know of the mountains? Moore wants good men. He'd discover you for what you are in a matter of minutes."

"And what am I, Bhol?" Turning, Chaque looked the other man in the eyes, his own surprisingly direct. "I've hunted and I know the area. I've spent as much time in the foothills as any of your vaunted guides. Just because I can't see the sense in making more money than I need doesn't make me a fool. There are other values. And I'll be frank, the adventure appeals to me. At least it will break the monotony."

The adventure and other things, Iduna Moore for one. A beautiful woman despite her mannish ways. A challenge to anyone like Chaque, with his enhanced self-esteem. He would fail, of course, and failing perhaps turn ugly, but that would be Moore's problem, not his.

"You know, Bhol, you don't really have much choice. Sirey probably recognized his folly and who else could you find? I think you should consider my offer."

"The decision is Moore's."

"True, but he has less choice than yourself." Chaque

smiled, confident of his position. "Of course you could wash your hands of the deal, but I don't think you'd like to do that. Right?"

Kinabalu said, "The pay is—"

"I know what the pay is. I want an increase of fifty percent."

"You'll take what's offered." The Hausi was firm. "And you'll have to talk Moore into accepting you. That's the best I can offer, Agus. Personally I don't think you stand a chance, but I won't speak against you."

A problem solved if the man agreed. Kinabalu felt an inward relaxation as Chaque nodded. The guide was replaced at least, which left the situation as before. He glanced at the ship. Two women were moving down the ramp, sisters he guessed, come to see the harvest. Wen Larz moved quickly toward them, smiling. The smile grew wider as others appeared, a couple with a small boy, a matron who sniffed disdainfully as she saw the town.

"So this is Shajok. I don't think much of it."

"You haven't seen the best yet, my lady." Larz bustled about as he collected his party. "That is yet to come. A vista of unequaled splendor which will stun the eye and fill the nostrils with almost unbearable delight. You have arrived at the best time. The fields are superb. Is there anyone else to take the tour? No? Then if you will all follow me, I will guide you to your accomodation."

To the rooms in the hotel of which he was the part owner. Later, they would take rafts and head towards the plains to camp and inspect the crop. Mile upon mile of ulumen, the plants all in full bloom, pods swollen with volatile oils. They would see a blaze of color stretching as far as the eye could reach. They would live, breathe, almost bathe in the perfume which hung over the area like a cloud.

Kinabalu ignored them, now looking at the ramp leading down from the open port. Zorya was talking to the handler, haggling over something he held in his hands, probably narcotics or a few semi-precious stones. Frend walked past, scowling, barely nodding a greeting. No one, obviously, had ridden Low. His mine would lack the cheap labor he'd hoped to obtain.

There seemed no reason to wait, and yet the Hausi lingered. Hoping.

Dumarest was late in leaving the ship. Shajok was a bad world. He could tell, almost smell it as he descended the ramp. A planet which had little in the way of industry, a backward world on which it would be hard to find work, to earn enough to build a stake. It was too easy to become stranded in such a place, waiting, working for food if work could be found at all.

A road led from the field towards the town, a cluster of beggars at its side. Crippled men and a few crones, their eyes dull, waiting, hoping for charity which would never come. Winter would kill them off like flies, but more would take their place in the spring.

The town itself had the grim appearance of having once been a fortress. The houses were fashioned of solid stone, the roofs sharply pitched, the windows narrow and barred. Only the pennons gave a touch of gaiety, long streamers of brilliant color, all pointing towards the distant loom of the mountains. Dumarest studied them, looking for emblems or symbols, seeing nothing but a jumble of hues.

The square was fringed with open-fronted shops selling a variety of local produce; dried meats on skewers, woven carpets, basket work. There were masses of fruit dried and pounded, then compressed into blocks, things of stone and wood and metal to be used in any household. A smith was busy at a forge, the sound of his hammer strident over the hum and bustle of the crowd. In a corner of the square a woman fashioned pottery.

She was old, stooped, hair a wispy tangle over small, bright eyes. Her arms were bare to the elbows, hands grimed with a grayish clay. Dumarest paused, picking up a bowl, looking at the material of which it had been made. A gray, stone-like substance which he had seen before.

As he set the bowl down the woman said, "Anything special you're after, mister?"

"A few words."

"For free?"

"For pay." He dropped a few coins into the bowl. "Do you fire this stuff?"

"No." She came towards him, wiping her hands. "It's ground levallite mixed with a polymer resin. Leave it stand and it sets as hard as a rock. Why?"

Dumarest said, "Did you have a boy working for you once?"

"I've had a lot of people working for me. They come and they go. Why should I remember?"

More coins made metallic sounds as they joined the rest in the bowl.

"His name was Leon Harvey. Young, slightly built, probably came from a village somewhere. His face was a little peaked, if you know what I mean. He wanted to move on and see the galaxy."

"I remember." Wispy hair straggled as she nodded. "He came to me starving and I gave him a bowl of stew. Made him work for it, though. He hung on and I fed him, gave him a little money from time to time. Then he upped and vanished."

"Just like that?"

"They come and they go," she said. "I guess he found his way around, then made his move. It happens."

"Did anyone come looking for him?"

"No—are you?"

"He's dead," said Dumarest flatly. "I was hoping to take word to his folks. He left a little something I thought they might like to have. Where can I find them?"

Her shrug was expressive. "Why ask me?"

"He worked for you. He must have talked, mentioned his home, his family. No?" Dumarest deliberately scooped the coins from the bowl. "Too bad—I guess we both wasted our time."

"Now wait a minute!" Her hand gripped his arm with surprising strength. "We made a deal."

"Sure, I pay and you talk, but so far you've done no real talking."

"There's nothing to talk about."

"No?" Dumarest's voice lowered, became savage. "A youngster, tired, hungry, working for barely nothing. A stranger, and you say he didn't talk? Hell, woman, he'd have to say something. You were the only one he knew."

"He was on the run," she admitted. "I guessed that, and was sure of it when he ducked under the counter one day. A group was passing, some men from the mountains, I think. He took one look, then ducked."

"Nerth," said Dumarest. "He told me he came from there. Where is it?"

"I don't know."

"A commune." Dumarest jingled the coins. "A village, maybe." He saw the blank look in her eyes. "The Original People then? Damn it, woman, don't you know your own world?"

For answer she took a mass of clay, slammed it on the counter, gouged it with her thumbs.

"Shajok," she snapped. "At least a part of it. Here are the plains, here the field, here the town. And here," her fingers mounded the gray substance into a range of peaks, "here are the mountains. And in the mountains—" Her hand slammed down, fingers clawing, digging, leaving deep indentations. "—valleys. Places where God alone knows what is to be found. Maybe people calling themselves by a fancy name. Maybe communes of one kind or another. I don't know. I'm no hunter and I've more sense than to stick my head into a noose. And, mister, if you'll take my advice, neither will you. See those flags? When they fall, get under cover and fast. Get into shelter and stay there until the wind blows again."

"Why?"

"Because, mister," she said grimly, "if you don't, you'll stop being human, that's why."

The interior of the tavern was dark, a place of brooding shadows in which men sat and talked quietly over their wine. Too quietly, but much about Shajok was less than normal. The flags, the town itself, the odd atmosphere of the field. A place besieged, thought Dumarest. Or, a place which had known siege. No wonder that Leon, after a taste of normal worlds, had sworn that he would never return.

Leon, whom the old woman had known in more ways than she had admitted. The boy must have turned thief to gain the price of his passage. But the money couldn't have come from her. Somewhere else then, that was certain, but from where? Home, perhaps. It would be logical for him to have stolen before running away, but in that case why work for the woman at all? And who were the men who had frightened him?

Questions which waited for answers, but at least one problem could be solved now.

Kinabalu grunted as Dumarest dropped on the bench at his side. "My arm!"

"Will be released as soon as I know why you have been following me."

"You noticed? Good. Is that why you came into this place?"

"It serves." Dumarest tightened his grip. "The answer. Why are you interested in me?"

"Please!" Sweat shone on the Hausi's face. "The bone—you will break it! All I wanted was to offer you employment."

"Your name?"

Kanabalu rubbed his wrist as he gave it. Beneath the fabric of his blouse he knew that welts would be forming, bruises which would make his flesh tender.

"Earl Dumarest," he said. "The handler gave me your name. I took the liberty of following you. That woman—why do you wish to find this place you call Nerth?"

"If she told you that, she must have told you the rest."

"And why not?" Kinabalu shrugged, fully at ease. "She knows me and knows of my discretion. Also, I was able to buy a few things for later delivery. Money, as you must know, has many uses."

"And?"

"I offer you the chance to earn some money. More, the chance to find what you are seeking. A fortuitous meeting, my friend. We must celebrate it in wine."

He ordered, waited as a girl poured, followed the movements of her hips with his eyes. A sensualist—or so a less observant man would have believed. Dumarest knew better. Knew also that a Hausi did not lie. He might not tell all of the truth, but his word was to be trusted.

"You followed me from the ship," Dumarest said. "Were you waiting for me?"

"No, not you, not as an individual. I hoped that someone would land who would fill a need. I think you are such a man. Some wine?"

Dumarest accepted the goblet. He said, dryly, "What's so special about this need of yours?"

"The need? Nothing. A job which any of a hundred men could do. To act as a guard and protector, to take care of a camp, to be able to survive in a hostile environment and, above all, not to be afraid. But the man who offers the employment is another matter. A man almost impossible to satisfy. On the face of it the commission was simple, to equip a small expedition into the mountains. To provide a raft, supplies, a guide, and a man. All is ready and waiting, only the man needs to be found. It could be that I have found him. You are open to a proposition?"

"I could be."

"That depends."

"On the pay, certainly, that is understood. But Jalch Moore will be generous."

"Moore," said Dumarest. "From where?"

"Does it matter?" Kinabalu sipped at his wine. "His

money is good even if his temper is short. But, if you are interested, he once mentioned Usterlan. I have never been to that world. Have you?"

"No."

"He is, I think, a little mad. The mountains are best left alone. You see, I am honest with you. I will add to my honesty—there is even a chance that you may be killed."

"By whom?"

"The wind, my friend, a fall in temperature, a vagary of heat. The mountains are dangerous for any raft. Thermals are unpredictable. A drop in the wind can create vortexes, a rise the same. And the local conditions are much of a mystery. Few venture deeply into the hills; some hunters, a scattering of prospectors, some seekers of gems. They leave, sometimes they return, sometimes they do not."

"And yet there must be caravans," said Dumarest flatly. "Traders who venture far to sell and buy."

"True."

"Are they proof against dangers?"

"No man is proof against death when it comes," said Kinabalu. "And it can ride on the wind."

"The wind," said Dumarest. "The pennons?"

"Signals, as the woman told you. While the wind blows all in the city are safe. If it should fall, there is nothing to worry about providing the calm does not stay too long. If it does—but why worry about such things? The wind never fails."

"But if it did?"

"Probably nothing." Kinabalu drank more wine. "A superstition, my friend, a sop to the credulous. A rumor circulated by tavern owners, for where can a man be sure of shelter and welcome if not in a tavern? But, seriously, the danger is exaggerated. Nothing could possibly come down from the mountains against the updraft from the foothills. But we digress. Are you interested in taking the position?"

A journey into the mountains, to look for—what? Nothing of interest, perhaps, but the expedition offered transportation and a chance to learn of what lay in the valleys the old woman had mentioned. They only way, perhaps. One he would have to take if ever he hoped to find Leon's home.

Dumarest said, slowly, "I'm interested, but I need to know more."

"The pay for example. The cost of a High passage, that I can promise. As for the rest—" Kinabalu finished his wine. "—that Jalch Moore will explain."

Chapter EIGHT

There was something odd about the man. He moved with the restless pacing of a hungry feline, his head jerking, hands twitching, eyes never at rest. His room at the hotel was littered with papers, maps, scrolls, moldering books, items of equipment. A dagger with an ornate hilt and engraved blade lay beside a small statuette of a weeping woman. In a crystal jar an amorphous something turned slowly, as if imbued with sluggish life. An illusion, the thing was dead, preserved, the motion the result of transmitted vibration.

"Dumarest," he said. "Earl Dumarest. From?"

"Vonstate."

"And before that?" The thin, angry tones sharpened a little. "The planet of origin, man. Where were you born?"

"Earth."

Dumarest waited for the expected reaction, the incredulity, the conviction of a lie. None came and he looked at Moore's hand, the small instrument it contained. A tonal lie detector, he guessed. The recorded vibrations of his voice tested by electronic magic to reveal the truth. An unusual tool for an explorer to carry.

He said, flatly, "And you? Usterlan?"

"Yes."

A lie. Dumarest knew the world despite what he had told the Hausi. The people of Usterlan were dark, their hair a kinked ebon, a protection against the fury of a sun radiating high in ultra-violet. His eyes slid to the woman sitting quietly beside the window. She wore masculine garb, her russet hair cropped short, her face devoid of cosmetics. A strong face, the bones promi-

89

nent, the lips firm, the bottom pouting a little. Her eyes were uptilted, a pale gray, the lids thickly lashed. Her hands were broad, the fingers long, the nails neatly rounded.

Iduna, Jalch Moore's younger sister.

"My lord," Bhol Kinabalu bowed a little, his hands extended, palms upward. "This is the man for whom you have been waiting. He will suit your requirements—if not, I must cancel the commission and answer to my guild."

An ultimatum, despite the appeal of the hands, the deferential bow. Moore grunted, dropping the instrument he carried, his hand moving towards the dagger, to snatch it up, to hurl it with a sudden gesture. A bad throw. Left to itself it would hit the wall close to where Dumarest stood, denting the plaster with its hilt.

He caught it, spun it to grip the point, threw it all in one fast motion. Metal tore as the blade ripped into the lie-detector, inner components ruined, its discharged energy flaring in momentary sparkles.

"Fast." The woman's voice was deep, musical. "A test, Jalch? If so, the man has passed. At least his reactions leave nothing to be desired."

"The instrument—"

"Is ruined, but he could have buried the steel in your throat had he wished." She rose, tall, a little imperious, the curves of her body betraying her femininity. "Have you been told what it is we want you to do?"

"No."

"No?" She frowned, glancing at the Hausi. Again Kinabalu spread his hands.

"I have explained the basic duties, my lady, but the details must come from you. To guard, to protect, these things are vague. Only a rogue would promise to deliver what he cannot supply." Pausing he added, "The guide?"

"Has been accepted."

"And this man?"

"We shall see. You may go." As the door closed behind the Hausi she said to Dumarest, "Have you been engaged in such employment before?"

"Yes."

"And yet you are not satisfied with what has been told you?"

"No." Dumarest met her eyes. "If I am to be efficient I need to know what dangers to anticipate. This enterprise you propose, what is it's purpose? To hunt? To map a region? To trade? To search for minerals?" The pale gray orbs did not flicker. "What?"

"Does it make a difference?"

"It could." Dumarest looked at the scattered maps, the scrolls, the moldering books. "How many will be on this expedition?"

"We two, the guide and yourself if you agree to join us."

"A small party."

"But large enough," snapped Jalch harshly. "Sister, let me explain." His hand touched a scroll, moved to a book, lingered on the statuette. "We are chasing a legend," he said abruptly. "Shajok is an old world and must have been settled many times. In the mountains are valleys which could hold the remnants of previous cultures. One of them could be the life that was native to this planet in ages past. From what I have been able to discover they were unique. You have seen the pennons?"

Dumarest nodded.

"You know their purpose?"

"A warning."

"The product of imagination—or so most insist. And yet, should they signal the ceasing of the wind there would be panic." Jalch moved restlessly about the room. "Why should that be if there is no danger? Superstition? I think not. The product, perhaps, of myths enlarged by active fears. Yet, each myth holds within itself the core of truth. Once there was a real danger. Once men were strangers here and had to fight in order to survive. The original people could still exist. If they do I hope to find them."

"The Original People?"

'The natives of this world." Pages rustled as Jalch opened a book. "Look at this, a report made by Captain Bramh centuries ago. He made an emergency landing close to the mountains and lost two-thirds of his crew to something he failed to describe. A local phenomenon he called it, which caused them to desert. And here, an item culled from the secret archives of Langousta. A ship which was forced to land on Shajok. A distress signal was picked up and a rescue operation mounted. They discovered the wreck, but found no trace of the crew and passengers it had carried. A mystery. Even the log was incomplete, food on the tables, everything as it should be, but of the people—nothing."

A book fell, a scroll rolled to the floor, a paper traced with lines of faded color was unrolled.

"And here, more proof if more were needed. A priest of the Hyarch sect was summoned to the bedside of a dying man. Under the seal of secrecy he was told of Shajok and the thing the man had found there. A form of life which—tell me, have you ever heard of the Kheld?"

Dumarest shook his head.

"A supposed creature of legend, the ancient writings mention them often. Things of strange powers and peculiar abilities. They have many names and have been recorded many times. Intangible life-forms which can grant powers beyond imagination to their owners. A name, and names change, but the basics remain. Here, on Shajok, we could find the Kheld."

Jalch moved towards the window, stood looking out at the bright pennons straining at their poles, his face traversed with bars of shadow.

"The Kheld," he whispered. "The Kheld!"

Iduna said quietly, "Earl, do you understand?"

A madman or a man obsessed, certainly not a man wholly sane. Jalch Moore had taken the stuff of rumor and built it into an imagined fact. Fragments of legend whispered in taverns and enhanced with the telling. Like the myths of vast accumulations of wealth to be found in hidden places, the deposited treasures of dying races, of imaginary pirates, of votive offerings.

Dumarest had heard them by the score—but this was something new. The mysterious beings which would grant to a man they acknowledged as their master the absolute fulfillment of his dreams and ambitions. And Jalch hoped to find them on Shajok.

A paranoid—that much was obvious from his use of the lie-detector. A mystic in his fashion, a primitive in his application of the crude ritual of the thrown dagger. Yet, he had money and equipment, and the urge to explore the hidden places of the mountains. The valleys, in one of which could be those whom Dumarest sought. The place from which Leon had come.

Nerth. A commune, perhaps, of the Original People. A chance he couldn't afford to miss.

They left two hours before dusk, lifting high and riding the wind, the note of the engine a soft purr as it fed power to the anti-gravity units incorporated in the body of the raft. It was a small, general purpose vehicle, the controls protected by a transparent canopy, the body open to the sky. A thing used to transport vats of ulumen oil, the structure redolent of the exotic perfume.

Jalch Moore handled the controls, the guide at his side, pointing at times to the mountains looming ahead. Dumarest sat in the open body, cramped by the bales of supplies and equipment, the woman at his side.

Without looking at her he asked, "What are you, his nurse?"

"His sister."

"I didn't ask your relationship. How long has he been insane?"

"Is he?" She moved to sit before him. The setting sun threw long streamers of light across the sky, their reflections catching her eyes and accentuating their color. "He has a dream, a conviction, and who are you to say that he is wrong? A man who claims to come from a mythical world. Earth!" She made the word an expression of contempt.

"I did not lie and you know it."

"Because of the instrument used by my brother?" Her shrug emphasized the shape beneath the masculine tunic. "It would have registered the same, no matter what you had said. We had waited too long, Jalch was getting too strained. A word misplaced, a doubt, and you would have been rejected. Another failure—and I did not want to see him disappointed again."

"So you fixed the detector. Was that wise?"

"You think I fear you, or any man?" Iduna smiled, white teeth flashing between the parted lips. "Or that I need a machine in order to determine character?"

"No," he admitted. "But your brother—"

"Could be wrong, I admit it. But, then again, he could be right. The pennons are there for a reason. There could be an unusual life-form still existing in the mountains. It could be what Jalch suspects. The old records could have told the basic truth. Legends," she mused. "How quickly they are built. A hero who has killed a handful of men is credited with a hundred, a thousand, a hundred thousand. A woman notorious for her passion has her prowess enhanced to ridiculous proportions. Old cities claimed to be veritable paradises have become, on inspection, the yearnings of lonely men. And yet the hero was real, the woman also, the cities exist. Are we to discount them because of exaggeration?"

"No, but equally, we need not consider them as true. There are other explanations."

"Such as?"

"Let us discuss what we know. The town could have once faced actual enemies, the construction of the houses proved that. Strong, squat, narrow windows which can be sealed with shutters. The pennons?" Dumarest gestured towards the mountains. "A simple warning system. Volcanic activity could have produced fumaroles, spilling a lethal vapor. A steady wind would have prevented it from reaching the city and plains. If there had been eruptions there could have been hot ashes, a reason for sealing the windows. Once indoors, the population would have been protected."

"And if there were no volcanoes?" Her eyes were steady on his own. "What then?"

"A native form of life, perhaps. Predatory birds attacking in swarms. Again the wind would have kept them at bay, the houses given protection."

"Neat," she commented. "You have an agile mind, Earl. Without any supporting evidence, whatsoever, you have provided two explanations for what you have seen."

"And your brother a third."

"No, his is the same as your second one. You differ only as to the nature of the assumed threat. Birds or Kheld, basically they are the same. And you forget the reports, the beliefs held by the inhabitants of the town. A fear of something handed down by generations. They have forgotten, but it could still exist."

He said, bluntly, "Do you believe in the Kheld?"

Her silence was answer enough. Dumarest looked at the sky, the mountains ahead. Already the foothills were thick with shadow, only the peaks retaining a sparkling brightness. The wind, steady until now, had fallen a little. Soon they would be flying into the dangers Kinabalu had mentioned, the upward gusts, the vagaries, the atmospheric turmoil.

Dumarest rose, moved carefully towards the two men at the controls. The raft, small, slow, heavily loaded, was unstable.

"We'd better land and make camp," he said. "Before it gets too dark."

"Not yet!" Moore was impatient. "We still have far to go."

"Chaque?"

The guide shrugged. "You are right, Earl. At night the winds are treacherous. In any case, we need to plan the next moves. There!" His arm rose, pointing. "There is a hollow and a stream. A good place to spend the night."

"A few more miles?"

"No," said Dumarest. "We land."

Iduna cooked, boiling meat and vegetables in a pot suspended over a fire built of scrub and brush; green wood which smoked and sent a wavering plume high into the air. There were tents, one for her, another for her brother, a third to be shared by Dumarest and the guide. The grounded raft formed the remaining side of an open-cornered square. The mouths of the tents faced the fire in the center.

Dumarest checked the raft, examining what it contained. Food and some water, enigmatic instruments in strong containers, a mass of papers and maps. Some large metal boxes were fitted with lids which would snap shut if anything touched the bottom, or closed by remote control.

Containers to hold the mysterious Kheld, he guessed, and wondered how Jalch Moore had estimated their size.

Other bales held trade goods; axes, knives, spades, picks, brightly colored fabrics and an assortment of cheap adornments. One box held weapons.

Dumarest picked a rifle from its nest and examined it in the dying light. A semi-automatic, the magazine holding twelve rounds. He checked the action, the bolt making a crisp clicking sound, then loaded it with cartridges from a box. A simple weapon, but one as effective as a laser if used with skill and far more reliable in the field.

"You like it?" Iduna had joined him.

"It will serve." Dumarest lifted it to his shoulder, felt the balance and heft, noted the way in which it fell into line.

"You've hunted." She had watched, pleased with what she'd seen. "For sport, or for a living?"

"For food." He glanced towards the tents. Jalch Moore and Chaque were in the one to his right, their silhouettes thrown sharply against the fabric by the light of a portable lantern. They were, he guessed, studying maps. "And you?"

"For specimens. I was the field supervisor for the Glatari Zoo before—well, never mind."

"Before your brother fell ill?" A delicate way to put it, but he had no desire to be cruel.

"Yes—you could call it that."

"What happened?"

"We were together on Huek. It is a strange world containing odd forms of life, most of them utterly vicious. The natives are little better, regressed savages who have forgotten any culture they might have owned. We paid tribute, but it wasn't enough. A party caught Jalch when I was away. When we found him—" She broke off, and he heard the sharp inhalations, sensed the remembered hurt.

"And?"

"They had—hurt him. His eyes, his hands, the things done to his flesh. Horrible! At first I thought he was dead, even hoped that he had died, but life still remained. It took a long time for him to recover—regrowths, slowtime, amniotic tanks, the best skills which money could buy. But his mind was never the same."

"And now he wants revenge," said Dumarest. "Is that it? If the Kheld are what he thinks, they could do what he cannot. Kill and destroy those who had hurt him. Is that why he wants to trap them?"

"I don't know."

"I think that you do." His voice was flat, hard. "A waste, Iduna. You shouldn't spend your life nursing the delusions of a sick mind."

"It's my life, Earl."

"Your life, your time, your money," he agreed. "When will the food be ready?"

"Soon. You'll eat with us?"

"No. I'm going to look around."

It was dark when he returned, stars scattered thinly in the sky, the crescent of a moon hanging low on the horizon. A large moon, silver as Leon had said. But this world wasn't Earth despite the moon, the limited stars.

The fire had died to a red glow and he squatted beside it, scooping some of what the pot contained into a bowl, eating with a spoon.

It was good food, rich in nourishment, tastily spiced. Chaque joined him as he reached for a second helping.

"What do you think, Earl?"

"About what?"

"This." Chaque's gesture embraced the tents, the raft, the darkness beyond. "Jalch Moore's crazy. He had me in his tent for hours, going over maps which almost fell apart as you touched them. I tried to tell him that the deep interior is anyone's guess, but he wanted facts and figures which can't be supplied. Tomorrow he wants to head into the Marasill Gap."

"And that is?"

"A fissure split between two mountains. You'll see it soon enough. A bad place for any raft. We'll have to fly high and pick our time." Leaning forward, he touched the rifle Dumarest had set down at his side. "There was no need for this. We're safe enough here."

"And later?"

"We could need the guns." Agus Chaque was grim. "There are some predators I'd rather not run up against, and the valleys could hold other kinds of danger. We don't know much about them, there's no need. We just let well enough alone. A few hunters gather skins and furs and some traders try to earn a living, but that's about all. On Shajok, the ulumen is the main crop and there is plenty of room in the plains."

Dumarest leaned back, watching the face limned in the dull glow of the fire, the lines, the shrewd eyes.

"You're a guide, Agus. You must know the area. Have you heard of a place called Nerth?"

"No, but that means nothing." Chaque threw a dried twig on the embers, blew it until it flared into a glow of flickering brilliance. "You're thinking of the boy," he said. "I heard about it. A youngster, right?"

"Yes."

"Too young, maybe, to have been fully initiated into his tribe. It happens. These valleys are closed and have their own ways. They use special names, even a special language at times That name, Nerth, it could have been the one used before initiation. Once he'd passed the test, he would have been told more." Chaque threw another twig on the fire. "Have you anything else to go on?"

Dumarest handed him the photograph.

"Not the Zelumini," said Chaque immediately. "Their women are all dark. Nor the Branesch, they never wear green." He hunched closer to the fire, squinting. "She couldn't belong to the Candarish because none of their women ever dress like that."

"The symbol on the wall," said Dumarest. "A fish. Do you know any commune who uses a decoration like that?"

"A fish? No." Chaque handed back the photograph. "Sorry, Earl, it seems I can't help."

Another dead end, but at least a little had been learned. Leon had been young—he would have been much younger when he had left home. A few years spelled the difference between a child and a man. The name—Chaque could be right. Had the fear of initiation sent the boy running from his people? The photograph, one taken by a wandering trader, perhaps? A caravan he had chased and joined?

Dumarest rose, turning, the rifle in his hands as the night was broken by a sobbing cry. A sound which rose to a scream, a frenzied shrieking.

"No! No! Dear God, no!"

Jalch Moore was tormented by nightmares. The flap of Iduna's tent opened and the woman, dressed in brief underwear, ran to comfort her brother. Her voice, oddly gentle, soothed the yammering cries.

"Did you see that?" Chaque drew in his breath. "Who would have guessed that under the clothes she wears lies such perfection? A woman who—"

"Is busy as you should be." Dumarest handed him the rifle. "We'll stand watches, turn and turn about. Wake me in two hours."

Chapter NINE

Dawn came with a flush of golden light, reds and ambers gliding the mountain peaks. The air was still, the smoke from the cooking fire rising straight as if drawn with a crayon against the sky.

At noon they reached the foothills, gliding over rugged terrain, naked rock showing through patches of scrub. Thickets of bushes, a few thorned trees, their branches twisted, ruby leaves edged with silver gray.

"Watch out for those," warned Chaque. "The spines carry poison."

They ate in mid-air, cold food washed down with water, and two hours later reached the Marasill Gap.

It was vast. The result, Dumarest guessed, of some ancient convulsion which had split the range, parting the hills as if with the blow of a gigantic axe. A narrow stream ran along the bottom, vanishing into an underground cavern, a blur of spray masking the entry. The walls were sheer, matted with vegetation. The air was heavy with a brooding stillness.

"Up," said Dumarest to Jalch at the controls. "Keep us high."

"Too high and we'll see nothing. There should be signs, a scar—"

"Which must have long since been overgrown. Up, man! Up!"

The raft lifted as Moore obeyed. Turbulence caught them as they topped the fissure, the vehicle veering, tilting as currents fought the controls. A moment and the danger had passed.

"Close!" Chaque wiped sweat from his face and neck. "If we had crashed then—" He broke off, shuddering. A long fall and no hope of survival. "I warned him against using the Gap, but he wouldn't listen."

"What lies beyond?"

"The valley of the Candarish. We'll camp there tonight."

It was small, sealed, the crest of the slopes topped by a tangled mass of thorn-bearing trees, the slopes themselves scored by terraced fields. On the level bottom horned cattle cropped at lush grass, the animals attended by boys. The village was a cluster of low houses built of stone and turf, the roofs gabled, the windows open slits which could be closed with curtains of leather.

A cluster of inhabitants came forward as the raft landed; men wearing rough garments of fabric and leather, the arms and shoulders of their jackets ornamented with tufts of colored fur. The women wearing long loose robes which trailed in the dirt, their heads covered, their faces veiled. Children, pot-bellied, dirty, their hair oily and lank, watched with enormous eyes.

"My friends!" Chaque jumped down from the raft and stood with both hands uplifted. "We come in peace, to trade, to bring gifts, to learn of your wisdom. Who is chief among you?"

"He stands before you." A wrinkled oldster, his eyes filmed with cataracts, his mouth wet with spittle, took one step towards the guide. "Are you known to us?"

"My gifts are my welcome. Tools of metal and cloths of bright colors."

"A trader." The old man nodded. "You are welcome. Come into my house and we shall talk."

He turned, walked away, Jalch Moore and the guide following him. From where she stood at Dumarest's side Iduna said, quietly, "The depths to which men can sink. They live in dirt and ignorance. Yet, only a relatively short journey away, lies the door to the stars."

"A door that can't be reached." Dumarest looked at the crest of the valley. The setting sun caught the leaves, turned them into a barrier of flame. "What does your brother hope to learn here?"

"A clue, perhaps a rumor, something to lead him to the Kheld." She jumped down from the raft. "Shall we walk a little? See what is to be seen."

Dumarest hesitated, looking at the men who stood, still watching them. They carried knives, but little else. One had a spear, another a crossbow, two more holding staves with rounded ends. From the feeding cattle came a soft lowing and, without a word, several women turned and headed towards them.

"Earl?"

It seemed to be safe enough, yet he knew that nothing could be taken for granted. A display of weapons might be taken amiss, yet to leave them behind was to beg for trouble.

A raft loaded with goods, four people, one a woman—a temptation the Candarish might not be able to resist.

"Go if you want, Iduna. I'll stay here."

She was back within the hour, her boots soiled, grime on her hands and face. Without a word she washed, using water from a canteen. Then, picking up a rifle, checked the load.

"Trouble?"

"Nothing I couldn't handle. A young buck thought he had the right to touch me."

"And?"

"I taught him differently." She smiled at his expression. "Don't worry about it, Earl. I only hurt his pride."

Perhaps the worst thing she could have done, as she should have known. Dumarest picked up his rifle.

"Stay here," he ordered. "Don't leave the raft until I return."

A fire had been lit before the houses, a great pile of brushwood which had been set to dry in the sun. It threw a ruddy, dancing glow in which the feeble, oil-burning wicks within the houses were dimmed to pale splotches of luminescence. Dumarest headed away from the fire, moving in a wide circle, eyes narrowed, ears tense for the slightest sound. He caught the pad of naked feet, the inhalation of breath and dropped, the rifle lifting.

The sounds died, but instinct warned him that he was not alone. He moved, carelessly silhouetted against the glow of the fire, dropping as something flashed out of the darkness towards him.

A spear which sliced the air above him, to land with a dull thud in the dirt behind. Another came, held by a pair of hands, the point stabbing where he lay. He rolled over, slammed the barrel of the rifle against naked shins, rose as the man fell, screaming.

"Earl?"

He ignored the woman's call. With his back to the fire, he retained his night-vision. Those who faced him would lose it. Against that he made a clear target, trusting to his speed to defeat any attack.

It came immediately. Two men, young, strong, faces bathed in the firelight, rose from the ground to leap towards him. One held a club, the other a staff. One attacking high, the other low.

Dumarest fired, aiming to kill, dodging as the staff aimed towards his skull. He fired again, running as the man fell.

"Iduna! Lift the raft! Lift it!"

"What's happening?" Chaque appeared at the door of a house, Jalch Moore peering over his shoulder. "What's going on?"

"Get to the raft! Move!"

Dumarest fired again as figures appeared on each side of the men. One fell, blood gushing from his mouth, his lungs ripped by the missile. The other, luckier, spun and fell nursing a broken shoulder.

"An attack?" Chaque was quick to grasp what was happening. "The raft, quickly!"

Dumarest covered them as they ran, men pouring from the houses to go after them, spear-points glinting in the firelight. One hit the guide on the forearm, cutting into flesh before the spear dropped free. Then he reached the hovering raft, had flung himself over the edge, Moore following close behind.

"Earl?"

"Coming!" Dumarest ran forward, emptying the magazine, throwing the rifle into the raft, leaping to grab the edge as it rose. Within seconds, he was aboard.

"What happened?" Moore looked stunned. "We were talking quietly when we heard a scream, then shots. You, Earl?"

"Yes."

"Have you gone mad? Do you realize what you did? I was about to learn something, a fact of great importance, and you ruined everything. Iduna! Return at once. We can smooth things out."

She said nothing, increasing their height, the fire now a distant point below.

Nursing his arm Chaque said, "Be careful, girl. Set us down as soon as you can. It would be stupid to run from spears and smash into a mountain."

They landed in a shallow dell in a place high and far from the valley, Iduna setting down the raft gently, guided by the blazing glow of a flare. By the light of a lantern Dumarest examined the guide's arm, finding only a shallow gash, binding it with materials taken from a medical cabinet. Jalch Moore was harder to please.

"You ruined everything," he accused. "Why did you have to fire at shadows? I trusted Hausi and I trusted my own convictions. In both cases, apparently, I was wrong. Or is there some reason why you don't want me to find the Kheld?"

Paranoia, trembling on the brink of complete insanity. Dumarest said, patiently. "It was a trap. They intended to surprise us. While you two were kept in conversation, we were to have been killed. I anticipated them, that's all."

"I don't believe it! Chaque?"

"It's possible," admitted the guide. "A small party carrying a fortune in goods, yes, it's possible. We wouldn't have been the first expedition to be lost in the mountains."

"But the information he was going to give me—"

"Words," said Dumarest. "Empty talk to keep you occupied. You underestimate the old man. He only told you things you wanted to hear."

"No!"

"You were with him for over an hour. What did you learn? Nothing. An entire hour—that alone made me suspicious. With people like the Candarish you trade first and talk afterwards." A thing Chaque should have known, but Dumarest didn't mention that. There was no room for recrimination in such a small party. "We'll eat," he decided. "Eat and rest. In the morning, we'll figure out what to do."

"There is no question about that," said Moore coldly. "We go on."

"To where?"

"Here!" Moore unfolded a map and tapped it with his finger. "Towards the east and upwards to this plateau. There is mention of it in the Eldrain Saga. There could be signs, symbols, evidence of the Kheld. The Candarish could have helped us—but it's too late for that now."

And perhaps too late for many things. Thwarted, Jalch Moore could turn vicious. Dumarest had noted the bulge under his blouse, the weight of a laser. Defied he would use it, killing without consideration, damaging the raft beyond repair, stranding them all. And Earl still had to find the object of his own search.

"If the Kheld exist we'll find them," he promised. "Now, Iduna, how about that food? Chaque, you'd better check the raft while I look around."

The dell was set on the summit of a pinnacle of stone, a dead vent which had become blocked and filled with wind-blown soil. The vegetation was springy, tough fibers matted into a compact whole. A place safe from any but airborne attack—one during which they would starve if anything happened to the raft.

Later, as he sat watching the wheel of the stars, Iduna came to sit beside him.

"Earl, it was my fault, wasn't it."

"The attack? No."

"I've been thinking. If I hadn't rejected that young buck—but I couldn't bear that he touch me."

"He was anticipating," said Dumarest. "If you hadn't fought he would have taken you, hidden you safely away somewhere."

"For later use," she said bitterly. "For him and his friends, and any other man who chose to use me. Animals!"

"You were strange. A female who dressed like a man. He'd probably never seen a woman's naked face before."

"Savages! Beasts!"

"Primitives," he corrected. "With a rigid culture and elaborate customs. You were outside the framework of his experience. Dress like a man—be treated like a man. Had we been killed and you kept alive, the women would have stoned you to death. To them you would have been unnatural. Dangerous. A thing to be destroyed."

She said, oddly, "Do you think I'm unnatural, Earl?"

"No."

"Some men do. They wonder what I look like when naked and hint that my interest lies only with other women. They don't understand."

A lonely child, perhaps. A father who had wanted only sons, an elder brother to emulate. And, if she had worked in the field as she had claimed, then the clothes would have been an elementary precaution to have diminished her attraction.

"It's late," he said. "You should get some rest."

"Sleep while you stand guard?"

"It's what I'm paid to do." He wished that she would leave him, sensing her feminine curiosity, the desire to probe. From behind the raft Chaque coughed, a harsh rasping sound in the stillness. Within the vehicle itself Jalch Moore turned, restless in his sleep.

"Earl!"

He turned as she came towards him, her arms lifted, embracing his neck, her hands pulling him close to press her lips against his own. For a moment he felt the demanding heat of her body. Then, as Jalch turned again, muttering, she drew slowly away.

"My brother—he needs me."

"Yes."

"Goodnight, Earl."

"Goodnight."

The night grew old. Dumarest woke Chaque to stand his turn at watch, then settled down to sleep. He woke with the sudden alertness of an animal, one hand reaching up to the shadow looming above, the other lifting the knife.

"Earl!" Chaque clawed at the hand which gripped his throat, recoiling from the knife which pricked his skin. "Don't! It's me!"

"What's wrong?"

"Something. I don't know what. Listen."

It came from above. A thin, eerie chittering, a peculiar stridation, like the rasp of chitinous wings. Dumarest rose, the rifle in his hands, eyes narrowed as he searched the sky. He could see nothing but the glitter of distant stars, the band of the galactic lens a pale swath low on the horizon. There was no wind, the air like glass.

"I was sitting, dozing I guess, then I heard it," whispered Chaque. "It swept over me and seemed to rise. But I could see nothing. Nothing!"

It came again, apparently nearer. A thin, nerve-scratching sound which filled the night with a peculiar menace. And then, as Jalch screamed in his nightmare, it was gone.

"Earl?" Chaque was shaken, his face ghastly in the starlight. "Was that one of the things we're looking for? One of the Kheld?"

"I don't know."

"If so, I hope we never find them." The guide glanced to where Iduna was soothing her brother. "We remain silent, right? We tell him nothing."

A sound in the darkness, an impression—what was there to report? Yet, to Jalch Moore it would be proof of the existence of what he sought. He would insist on remaining in the dell, setting up his traps, waiting, risking all their lives. And Dumarest had no interest in finding the Kheld.

The days became routine. Waking to eat, to drift deeper into the mountains, to camp at night, to eat again. Twice more they found isolated communities, trading, listening to vague rumors. A mass of conflicting and contradictory stories which sent them on a random pattern of search. And daily, Jalch became more deranged.

"We'll find them," he muttered, crouching over his maps. "Here, perhaps? Or here? We must head for the higher peaks." He snarled like an animal as Chaque protested. "You claim to be a guide—why are you so irresolute?"

"Because I have a regard for my skin. The higher we go, the greater the danger. The winds—"

"Do you suggest we return?"

"No." Dumarest leaned over the map. It was rough, inaccurate, the product of speculation and surmise, but some things he recognized. "Here." He rested his finger on a valley, one to the east. "We could try there."

"A valley, we need the heights!" Jalch Moore was impatient. "The fools know nothing. We must climb high and search the peaks."

They lifted too soon in the day, thermals catching the raft, sending it spinning dangerously close to an overhang.

"He'll kill us," said Chaque as he clutched at the raft's edge. "Earl, can't you take over? Stop him?"

"He's a good pilot." That, at least, was true. Jalch could handle a raft, and to argue now was to invite disaster. Dumarest leaned over the edge, looking below, seeing a snarled jumble of crevasses, ridges, naked stone wreathed with massed thorn. He felt the presence of the woman at his side, the warmly soft impact of her arm against his own.

"What are you looking for, Earl? What do you hope to find?"

"Here?"

"Anywhere. You're a traveler, always moving, always looking. Why?"

"Why do you hunt specimens in the field?"

"A job."

"Which could be done as well by others." He turned to face her, catching the speculation in her eyes. "To each their own, Iduna. You have your ways, I have mine."

"You're hard," she said. "Hard and cold. While I wish I didn't, I do admire you. Envy you a little, perhaps. Has any woman ever owned your heart?"

She frowned as he made no answer, recognizing his silence for the barrier it was. Since the night on the dell, she had made no further advances and he had invited none. A thing which perturbed her, offended her femininity.

"You have loved," she decided. "And you have been loved in turn. What happened, Earl? Did she die? Did you leave her? Does some lonely woman sit on some world, waiting for you to return?"

"Does some man wait for you?"

"No, or if they do they are fools. But no man has ever been really close to me. Always there is something, a barrier, between those who want me and those whom I want." She leaned a little further over the edge of the raft. "What was that? An animal?"

There was nothing, or if there had been it had vanished. A diversion, Dumarest guessed. Something to break the trend of the conversation, to shift it from what she could have considered dangerous ground. He felt the raft shift a little as Chaque came towards them.

"Iduna, you've got to stop him." His head jerked to where Jalch sat at the controls. "He wants to climb to the summit of the range, then quest along the entire area. He's mad."

"He is in charge of this expedition," she said coldly.

"Even so, he is mad. The winds—it has never been done before. He doesn't understand and won't listen. Please, you must make him be more cautious. I—" Chaque broke off, cursing as the raft veered. "The fool! Why won't he listen?"

Dumarest moved back from the edge.

"You're the fool," he said sharply. "You're unbalancing us. Get up to the front, quickly!"

It was too late. As the guide moved an updraft, combined with eddys thrown from the flank of the mountain, cojoined to create a turbulence which spun the raft and sent it crashing against a ridge. A near miss, only the bottom was affected, but it was enough.

"Quickly!" Dumarest gripped a bale, threw it over the edge, snatched at another. "Lighten the raft before we drop too low."

Drop into a natural chimney, the mouth of a natural funnel, the vortexes it would contain. The crash had ripped some of the anti-gravity conductors from their housings. Overloaded, most of its lift gone, the raft tilted as it dropped, spinning hopelessly out of control.

"Move!" Dumarest flung another bale over the side, followed it with some of the large metal boxes, a crate of instruments.

"No!" Jalch abandoned the controls, lunging from his seat into the body of the raft, hands clawing at the cargo. "You can't! I need these things! I need them!"

Dumarest struck him once, a hard blow to the jaw which sent the man sprawling and stunned. As Jalch fell Dumarest lunged for the controls, gripped them, fought to steady the raft which was now pitching and tilting. He heard Chaque cry out, saw the side of the chimney coming close. Then, they had hit with a grinding impact.

"The load—dump it!"

Chaque obeyed as the raft veered from the rock, lifting a little, dropping as it hit a mass of cold air, again hitting the slope of the mountain. It turned almost on edge, skidded down a mass of rock, hurtled into space to slam against a boulder lower down. Metal ripped with a thin squeal, and a gush of acrid smoke rose from the controls. Bared wires touching, energy short-circuited, the engine itself falling silent as they fell.

Fell to land in a shallow ravine, the impact cushioned by matted vegetation, which lay in and around the wreckage of the raft.

Chapter TEN

Chaque groaned, rising to nurse his arm, his head. The skin had broken over one temple, blood smearing his cheek. His hair was filled with torn leaves and his blouse was torn at the back and side.

"Earl? Earl, where are you?"

"Here." Dumarest stepped towards the guide. Bright flecks showed on the scratched plastic of his tunic and his hands were grimed. "How are you?"

"My head!" Chaque felt it, wincing as he probed his temple. "Nothing broken, I think, but it aches like hell."

"Can you move?" Dumarest watched as the man took a few steps. "Good. Let's find the others."

Iduna lay to one side, her face pale, a cheek stained green and brown from dirt and leaves. She stirred as Dumarest touched her, his hands searching for broken bones. One leg of her pants had split, the cream of a thigh showing through the vent. As his hands moved over her waist she sighed and opened her eyes.

"Earl. What happened?"

"We crashed." His fingers ran through her cropped hair, finding a bump, but nothing more serious. "We were lucky."

"And Jalch?"

Jalch Moore was dead. He rested high on a slope, cradled in the twisted branches of a thorn, ruby leaves framing his face, silver spines imbedded in his cheek, his neck. His eyes were open, glazed, his hands raised, the fingers curved as if, at the last, he had tried to clutch something and hold it close.

112

A dream, perhaps, a forgotten happiness. At least his nightmares were ended.

"Jalch!" Iduna strained against Chaque's holding arm. "I must go to him."

"Be careful, girl," snapped the guide. "Touch those spines and you'll regret it."

"But my brother—"

"Is dead. His neck is broken." Dumarest looked back towards the ruin of the raft. "He must have been thrown out before we crashed. We'd better look around and see what we can find."

"But, Jalch? You're not leaving him like that?"

"Why not? I told you, he's dead. What does it matter to him where he lies?" Dumarest stepped before her as she tore herself away from Chaque's hand. "You want to rip yourself to shreds trying to get him down? And then what? Can we bring him back to life? Have some sense, woman! We have more to worry about than Jalch."

She said, unsteadily, "I suppose you're right, Earl. It's just that, well, we were so close."

And now she was alone. Dumarest watched her as they moved down the slope. There were no tears, but her face was hard, a firmly held mask. Inside she could be weeping, but if she was, nothing showed.

"Here!" Chaque had found a metal box.

"Leave it. We need food and the medical cabinet. Some fabric too, if you can find any. And the rifles." Dumarest looked back at the dead man, at the laser he carried beneath his arm, but the risk was too great. "Look for the rifles. Spread out and carry what you find back to the raft.

It wasn't much; a bolt of fabric, some compressed fruits, a crate of broken instruments, a canteen. Dumarest lifted it and found it to be half-full.

"We could look again," suggested Chaque. "Spend the rest of the day searching."

"No." The area was too wide, the vegetation too thick. The bales and other things had been scattered when the raft had almost overturned.

Iduna said, "Can't we repair the raft?"

"Impossible." Dumarest had examined it. The engine was ruined, the conductors ripped and useless. "And we can't hope for rescue. Chaque, have you any idea of how to get out of these mountains?"

"Without flying, no," admitted the guide. "But I can tell you what to expect; crevasses we won't be able to cross, walls we won't be able to climb. Predators and thorns and blind canyons. Earl, we need those rifles!"

"Look for them if you like, I'm moving on."

"Moving on?" The woman was incredulous. "But we need rest and—"

"We're bruised," he said shortly. "Later, we'll be stiff. The longer we wait around here the harder it will become." Dumarest unrolled the bolt of fabric and cut off a length with his knife. "Wrap this around your leg—it will protect your thigh. You too, Chaque, cover those rents."

As they worked, Dumarest went to the raft. With his knife he levered off a distorted panel, reached inside and ripped loose a handful of wires. The control chair was covered in thick plastic. He cut it free, trimmed a small oblong piece and punched holes in either end. Using some of the wire for thongs, he made a sling shot.

He tested it with a stone, sending the missile to land high on a slope.

"Here." He handed the woman his knife and the rest of the plastic. "Make a pouch and some gloves. Nothing fancy, just to protect our hands from thorns."

She looked blankly at the articles. "How—"

"Cut thin strips from the plastic to use as thread. Use the point to make holes. The fabric will make a pouch and strap to support it. Chaque, help me get some metal off the raft."

They managed to get three strips, each about a yard long, an inch wide, a quarter thick. Crude swords without point or edge, but having mass which could be used as a club. The thorn trees were too spined, the branches too twisted, the wood too hard to be of use.

Dumarest tore a panel from the wreck, stabbed holes in it, cut it to shape. The guards were crude, but they would protect the hand from anything running along the rough blades.

"Cutlasses," said Chaque. "Or machetes—but they haven't an edge."

"Find me a grindstone and I'll give you one. That, or an anvil and hammer."

"Why not ask for a radio while you're about it. And a raft all set and ready to go?" Chaque lifted one of the weapons, swung it, grunted as the end dug into the soil. "The hunters use high-powered rifles and lasguns," he commented. "We haven't even got a decent sword. Earl, we've got to face it. We haven't a hope in hell of getting back alive."

"Why not?" Dumarest looked at the guide, his eyes cold. "We can walk. We can navigate by the sun and stars. As long as we keep going, we'll get somewhere."

"Not in the mountains. You don't know what they're like and—" his voice lowered, "that thing could come back. You remember? The one in the dell."

"We'll worry about that when it happens," said Dumarest. "Ready, Iduna? Let's go."

He led the way, picking a trail up the southern end of the ravine, reaching the top to look down at an expanse of thorn which fell gently to a sharp rim. An almost solid barrier of wood and spine which nothing living could easily penetrate. He turned to the left and followed the edge of thorn to where it met a jutting outcrop; a sharp wedge of stone which rose almost sheer, until it sloped up and back towards the flank of the mountain.

"A dead end." Chaque's voice betrayed his fatigue. "The mountains are full of them. We'll have to go back, Earl, and try the other direction."

Miles of distance and hours of time wasted to no purpose. Energy squandered and fatigue enhanced. Dumarest looked at the wall before them, noting its cracks, small fissures, clumps of vegetation.

"We'll climb," he said. "Move up and around."

"And, if beyond, there is more thorn?" Chaque slashed at the ruby leaves with his metal bar. "A slip and we could fall into it. Once trapped, we could never escape."

A chance which had to be taken. Dumarest looped a wire around the handle of his sword and slung it from his neck. The pouch, now filled with selected stones, followed. The gloves he tucked under his tunic and, without hesitation, began to climb. Twenty feet up he halted and looked down.

"Use my hand and footholds. Iduna, you come next. Chaque, you take the rear."

"I'm no climber, Earl."

"You'll manage. Just look up and ahead, never down."

Dumarest climbed higher as they followed, fingers digging into cracks, boots resting on tiny ledges, the clumps of vegetation. One yielded beneath his weight. He heard Iduna gasp as dirt showered about her, Chaque's muffled curse as a stone hit his injured temple.

"Earl?"

"It's nothing. Just keep moving."

Up another fifty feet, and then he met an overhang under which he sidled like a crab. A gust of wind swept over the thorn, stirring the leaves so they flashed with changing ruby and silver, spines lifting as if eager for prey.

The curve of the outcrop was smooth, worn with wind and weather. Dumarest edged around it as far as he could go, then looked up and down. Ten feet below on the far side of the curve errosion had caused a mass of stone to fall, leaving a scooped hollow above a ledge almost four feet wide. A safe place to rest if they could reach it, and there was only one way to do that.

To swing, to jump, to land and, somehow, to maintain balance. To slip was to fall and land among the thorn.

"Earl? Is something wrong?" The woman sounded anxious.

"No. Just hold on."

Again, Dumarest examined the curve. It was bare, unmarred aside from a narrow fissure which ran in an almost horizontal line. Reaching behind him Dumarest lifted the crude sword from his neck, probing ahead with the tip of the blunt blade. It penetrated an inch then, as he turned it, slid within the fissure for half its length. He hammered it home with the heel of his hand and then, gripping it, swung from his holds, dropping, landing with a thud on the ledge to teeter on the very brink.

A moment of strain as muscles and reflexes fought the pull of gravity. Then he was safe, dropping on all fours, his lungs pumping air.

"Earl?" Iduna was above, her face pale, strained as she looked at where he stood. He saw her lips tighten as he told her what to do.

"Earl! I can't! I—"

"You've got no choice!" He was deliberately curt. "Grab the bar, swing and let go. I'll catch you before you can fall. Hurry! Don't think about it, just do it!"

She hit the edge of the ledge, swayed and gasped as he swung her to safety. Chaque followed, unexpectedly agile. Without pause Dumarest led the way down to where piled dirt made an easy slope, leading past the thorn to a ridge running south, a rugged expanse dotted with scrub.

The far end terminated in a crevasse impossible to cross. Chaque looked at it, his eyes bleak.

"I told you, Earl. These mountains are difficult to fly over and impossible to traverse on foot. We'll never make it."

"You give up too easily." Dumarest looked around, studying the vegetation, the lie of the land. Already the day was ending, reflected light flaring from the peaks, the crevasse filled with somber shadow. "We need to find water. My guess is that it's over there."

"How can you tell?" Iduna followed his pointing hand.

"No thorn—it needs arid conditions. And see how those leaves reflect the light? What vegetation is that, Chaque?"

"Frodar—if it were the season there would be fruits."

"And fruit needs water." Dumarest took the rough sword from the woman. "Let's go and find it."

They reached it at dusk after fighting their way through a cluster of thorn, hacking a passage with the strips of metal. A thin stream ran between high banks to widen into a pool a few feet across. Dumarest held the others back as they lunged towards it.

"No. We'll drink and wash lower down. I don't want to leave our scent."

Later, when he had immersed his entire body in the stream, laving his clothing and boots, he returned to the pool. Moving around it he set snares made of looped wire, hammering pegs into the ground to hold them fast.

"Predators," said Iduna. "Of course, they have to live on something. Small game, Earl, is that what you're hoping to catch?"

"Small or large, we need to eat." Dumarest took her by the arm and led her from the pool to higher ground. Chaque, a blotch in the darkness, followed, stumbling with fatigue.

"Do we need to go so far?"

"Too near and our scent will warn off the game. How's your head?"

"Bad." Chaque grunted as he felt his temple. "I wish we'd found the medical cabinet. I could do with something to ease the pain,"

"Try to sleep," said Dumarest. "It will help."

"And you, Earl? Don't you ever sleep?" Iduna dropped to the ground as they reached a point well away from the water and the snares. "God, I'm tired. The way I feel, I could rest for a week. Do you think we'll trap anything?"

Two creatures were in the snares when they looked in the morning. Small things the size of rats, their skins a dull gray, matted with fur, oily to the touch. Dumarest skinned and cleaned them, cutting them into portions with his knife. Iduna looked distastefully at the pieces he held out to her.

"Aren't we going to cook them?"

"Raw meat gives more nourishment than when it's cooked. Chew it slowly and eat as we travel."

"Is there any point?" Her eyes were dull, her voice listless. "Isn't it only putting off the inevitable? What hope can there be, Earl?"

"There's hope. A valley should lie to the east and south. There could be people. If we reach it, we can survive."

"Among beasts like the Candarish?"

"Among people. Now take the food and do as I say." His voice hardened as she made no effort to take the scraps. "It's your choice, woman. Eat or starve!"

They followed the stream until it petered out, climbed a ridge and crossed a small plateau. That night they huddled in the shelter of a clump of shrub, moving on foodless, the next day. A flight of birds appeared, wheeling. Dumarest knocked down three with his sling, losing one as it fell into thorn, managing to save the others. They were mostly beak and feather, the flesh gritty, hard to chew, distasteful to swallow.

The thorn thickened, met in a barrier a hundred yards thick, thinning on the other side to a rise topped by pinnacles of naked stone. A barrier which ran to either side, as far as the eye could see.

"From where he stood on Dumarest's shoulders Chaque reported, "It's no good, Earl. We'll have to go back."

"Back?" Iduna had slumped, sitting with shoulders bowed, her face drawn with fatigue. "You mean we've done all this for nothing?"

She was dispirited, on the verge of defeat. To return now would be to break her will to survive. Dumarest frowned as the guide dropped to the ground beside him. The mountains were like a maze, promising paths ending in tormenting barriers. He watched as a gust of wind dried riffled the spined leaves.

A wind which blew from behind them, sweeping from the rising ground. If it lasted, they would have a chance.

Chaque watched as Dumarest knelt, fretting a piece of the gaudy fabric into a mound of scrapped fibers.

"If you're thinking of fire, Earl, it won't work. The thorn is slow to burn."

"Not the wood, the leaves." Dumarest selected a stone from his pouch, struck the back of his knife against the flint. Sparks flew, some settling on the tinder, smoldering to burst into minute flame. "Get me something to burn. Hurry!"

There was grass, sun-dried, still containing sap but releasing heat as well as smoke. Scraps of branch followed, some ruby leaves which Dumarest tore free with his knife and gloved hands.

"Keep building the fire," he ordered. "Make it as hot as you can."

As Chaque crouched, coughing over the glowing embers, Dumarest examined the barrier. To walk through it was impossible, but there had to be room at the foot of the boles and the small animals must have made trails. He found one, another much larger, and he dropped to stare into it. The edges were thick with leaves, the opening low. Smoke passed him, blown by the wind, streaming into the winding tunnel.

Dumarest piled fire into the tunnel mouth, watching as the silver spines curled and fell, the ruby leaves smoldering and releasing an acrid smoke.

Without the wind the fire would die, the leaves and wood proof against the flame. But, as the gusts strengthened, the flames grew, streaming back into the tunnel, sharp poppings coming from within. Iduna looked up as Dumarest tore the rest of the fabric into strips.

"Earl?"

"Wind these around your head and neck. Make certain that no flesh is exposed. You too, Chaque."

The wind died, the fire with it, thin streams of smoke lifting to die against the azure of the sky. The ground was barely warm, but the rim of spined leaves had gone leaving only blackened ash.

Muffled from head to foot Dumarest thrust his way into the tunnel, the crude sword extended, body flat, elbows and knees edging him forward. Twenty yards and the effect of the fire ended. But here, deep in the barrier, the leaves were relatively high above the ground. The gloom was intense, sunlight hidden by the massed leaves, the air filled with a dim ruby suffusion.

He moved on, his body making a passage the others could follow, the leaves thickening as he neared the far side of the barrier. He felt the rasp of leaves on his back and shoulders, spines tearing at the plastic, but unable to penetrate the protective mesh. Some caught at the fabric around his head, tore the material around his eyes.

He rolled, thrashing, moving on, the metal strip probing. It touched wood, something which squealed and ran. Then he had broken through, to roll, to turn and slash at the opening, to help the others through.

"We made it!" Chaque stood still as Dumarest unwound the fabric from around his head. The material was thick with broken spines. "Earl, we made it!"

A trick they couldn't repeat. The fabric was ripped, useless, loaded with poison. Dumarest left it where it lay as he headed on, up the rise, past the sparing pinnacles of stone to where a shallow canyon ran between sheer cliffs. It was open at the far end, giving a vista of sky and fleecy cloud. A bleak place, dotted with huge boulders, the ground rough and patched with thorn and scrub.

They were half-way along it when the predator attacked. It came from behind a boulder, long, low, limbs tipped with sickle-like claws, the tail knobbed with a spine, the head plated, the jaws filled with curving fangs.

Dumarest saw it, a drab-colored shape which sprang from the top of a boulder, its fur the bleak reddish gray of stone. A glimpse only, but it was enough to save his life, to send him lunging forward, to fall, his side numbed by the blow which had ripped away the pouch of stones. He rose as the beast landed.

"Iduna! Get behind a boulder! Chaque! On guard!"

The guide was slow, fumbling with his metal strip, his face pale, mouth gaping. If the beast had attacked him he would have fallen an easy prey, but the creature had mind only for its original target.

It crouched, a dry hissing coming from its open mouth, the knobbed tail lashing. The plates of bone armoring its head provided a defence against the thorn. The eyes shone behind transparent lids, deep-set, overhung with bony ridges. The shoulders were broad, the body tapering, thick fur matted over more natural armor. A wedge of savage destruction intent on the kill.

"Chaque, help him! Help Earl!"

Dumarest ignored the woman, concentrating on the beast. He held the crude sword in his right hand, feet poised, ready to leap in any direction. Had he the time he would have used the sling to try and blind the gleaming eyes, but there was no time.

Without warning it sprang. It lunged forward with an explosion of energy, dirt lifting beneath the claws of its rear legs, front paws extended, the claws gleaming like ivory. Dumarest darted to his right, the blade lifting, falling as the creature passed, the metal bar slamming against the sloping side. A true sword would have cut, dragged, severed tendon and bone, opened veins and arteries to release a fountain of blood. The bar hit, bruised, the jar stinging Dumarest's hand and arm.

The beast landed, hissing, turned to spring again. A thrown stone bounced from its shoulder as it left the ground, a missile too small and too weakly thrown to be of use. Dumarest dropped, ducking, feeling the touch of something on his head as he swung the bar at a rear leg with all his force.

A crippling blow, the best he could do. If he hoped

to kill the beast, first it must be slowed down. He rose, blood streaming from his lacerated scalp, the tip of a claw having sliced the skin as if it had been a razor. He threw the bar from his right hand to his left, lifting the knife from his boot, holding it sword-fashion, thumb to the blade, the point upwards.

A knife-fighter's hold, giving the opportunity to either slash or stab.

"Chaque! Move in! Hit when you can, but watch out for the tail!"

The guide said nothing, standing, the bar held limply in his hand.

"Chaque, damn you! Do as I say!"

There was no time to wait, to see if the man would help. Dumarest tensed, crouching a little, anticipating the spring. The damaged rear leg would throw the beast to his left, lessening the distance, the height. The target would be small and a mistake would cost him his life.

He rose as the beast sprang, his left arm extended, the bar held like a sword, firmly rigid. His aim was good. The blunt tip vanished between the gaping jaws, plunged into soft, internal tissues, driven deeper by the creature's weight. Fangs rasped as they bit, scraping as they ran along the metal to jar against the hilt. Dumarest released it, dropped, feeling the wind made by raking claws as stabbed upwards at the unprotected stomach.

Blood showered as he dragged the bar free, hot, smoking, sliming his face, his body, mixing with the dirt which plumed from beneath scrabbling claws.

The armored head turned, blood gushing past the bar, fangs denting the metal as they fought the cause of its pain. Pain which filled the beast's universe, which sent it twisting to one side, entrails hanging from the cut in its flesh. It was dying, as good as dead. Yet, life and the feral desire to kill still remained.

Dumarest yelled as Chaque suddenly ran forward.

"Don't! Keep clear, man! Keep clear!"

The guide ignored him, lifting his bar, aiming for the

point before the rear legs. He hoped, perhaps, to break the back.

A dangerous point to hit, a position which placed him within reach of the lashing tail. It struck as the bar landed, the knobbed end, moving like a whip, smashing against Chaque's side and his spine, knocking him down to scream as a clawed foot ripped at his body.

To scream and writhe as Dumarest lunged forward, the knife lifted, falling like a glint of silver as it plunged into the creature's heart.

"Earl!" Iduna came running towards him. "I tried to help," she panted. "I threw stones. Earl—is it dead?"

"Yes."

"And Chaque?"

Chaque was dying. He looked up from a face smeared with dirt and blood, his eyes filled with agony. His back had been broken, the claws had bared the bone of his ribs, revealed the spongy mass of his lungs. Already they were filling, drowning him in his own blood.

"Earl!" He coughed, spat a mouthful of crimson. "Too slow," he whispered. "I was too slow."

"You killed it." A lie, but perhaps it would give comfort. "You saved my life, Agus."

"I'm glad, Earl." Incredibly, the man smiled. "Now, at least, you'll have something to eat. And Earl, the woman—" He coughed again, spraying blood. "The woman, Earl, she—"

"He's raving." Iduna stooped, her hands touching the tormented body. "It's all right, Chaque," she said gently. "It's all right."

"The pain!" His face twisted. "God, the pain!"

Agony which bathed him like a flame. Torn nerves and sinews relaying their message, now that the shock had passed. Agony which could last for minutes, each second an eternity of suffering.

"Earl! Please! The pain! For God's sake help me! I can't stand the pain!"

"All right, Agus," said Dumarest gently.

And drove his knife into the heart.

Chapter ELEVEN

Phal Vestaler, High Rememberancer and, by virtue of that office, Head of the Council, stood before the Alphanian Altar and communed with the past. A solemn moment which he stretched to the full before turning, hands upraised, to face the score of boys now undergoing initiation.

A portentious moment in their lives—after the full completion of the ceremony they would never be the same. The days of boyhood would be over. They would adopt the raiment of a man, undertake the duties of a man, accept the responsibilities. They would marry the women chosen to be their mates and take full part in the ceremonies. They would listen and they would learn and, in due time, they would teach. So it had been from the beginning.

Vestaler looked at them from where he stood on the low dais. Already they showed signs of the adults they would soon become. Faces young but solemn, old for their age, the eyes tense, the lips firm. If they knew fear, they hid it well.

And they must know fear—the terror of the unknown, rumors enhanced by whispers, imagination multiplying dire fancies. They knew it as he had known it, now so long ago. Then, as they did now, he had stood trembling on the brink of mysteries, half-tempted to run, only the shame of displaying his fear holding him fast.

Others had not been as strong. They had worn the yellow until they had been given a second chance. And even then—

Vestaler mentally shook himself, recognizing the

trend his thoughts were taking. To brood was useless, to regret the same. None had accused him, yet he felt his guilt. He should have known. To him the responsibility—to him the blame.

"Master!"

A junior was at his side, the carved bowl filled with water in his hands. A discreet reminder that time was passing and there was still much to do. The instruction, the warning, the blessing. And, afterwards, the journey to the place of ordeal. His voice held the tones of an organ.

"You are at the threshold of becoming men. To be a man is not simply to grow. A man is not a large child. He is a person who has proven his right to exist, to help, to serve. He has gained the right to perpetuate his line in the production of children. Yet, how to prove that you have reached the state of manhood? To take your rightful place among us? To share as all share in the fruits of the soil, the common labor?"

A pause as a gong throbbed, soft thunder accentuating his words, engraving them on memory.

"You are to be taken to the high places. There, you will be left in solitude for the duration of the night. Those who are weak of will, have guilt in their hearts, are unfitted to join the community as men, will not return. If any of you hold doubt as to your fitness, now is the time to speak."

Another pause, another beat of the gong. Those who spoke would be removed, given further instruction, another chance. Men grew old at different speeds—sometimes they never achieved true maturity.

Now it was time for the blessing. He gave it, dipping his hands in the scented water, scattering limp droplets. A symbolic rain coupled with an actual washing, an act which absolved him and all from any taint of guilt.

Should any fail they would be innocent of blood. And some would fail. Always, there were some who failed.

The gong throbbed for the last time, soft thunder

echoing within the chamber, dying in murmurs as it was muted by the artifacts, the walls. In answer to the signal the doors opened, armed men standing outside, the escort waiting to conduct the initiates.

Vestaler watched them go, looking from a secluded window. The parents also would be watching, remaining equally unseen, but others had no reason to hide. Men grown old and others new to the estate. Boys almost touching the age of selection, and others with still many years to go.

Boys and men, but no women, no girls. They had their own ways, and each at such times remained apart.

At the side of the column Varg Eidhal set the pace. He was a big man, prone to easy laughter, one fond of sport and wine. The ceremonies irked him, and he was bad in the fields—two things which had persuaded the Council to grant his request to patrol the far slopes.

It was a job he liked. There was opportunity to hunt and to escape routine duty. Time had given him command and mostly, he enjoyed the life. Only at times like this did he tend to become short with his men.

"Keep in step there!" he rapped. "Armand, lengthen your stride! Lambert, shorten yours! That's better. Left! Left! Left, right, left!"

One of the boys stumbled.

"Easy, lad." Eidhal was unexpectedly gentle. "Just keep your head up and your eyes straight ahead. Just remember that tomorrow, you'll be a man."

A man or a memory—a tear in a woman's eye, a hardness in a man's expression. Eidhal didn't like to think about it.

The houses fell behind as they marched through fields thick with well-tended crops. A figure rose to stare towards them, a man dressed in gray, his face blank, his hands hanging limply at his sides. A ghost, a thing Eidhal didn't like to look at or think about. He ignored the call from the figure which came shambling towards the column.

"Wait! I wanna come. I wanna . . ."

The gray figure stopped, one hand lifting to finger its

mouth. The hand fell as, like an automatum, it turned away to resume the endless task of weeding.

"Sir!" One of the boys had heard the call. "Why can't he—"

"Keep moving, boy!" Eidhal snapped the command. "Later, you will understand."

The fields passed and now the end of the valley could be seen in greater detail. Slopes narrowing, rising, the ruby of thorn thick at the crests. A path led upwards toward the high places, kept clear by continual labor, another of the gray ghosts vanishing as they approached.

The pace was slower now. The sun, while low, was still high enough to grant a little slack and Eidhal was not a man who took pleasure in the discomfort of others.

Armand came towards Eidhal as he called a halt on a level space.

"You want me to go ahead Varg? Just in case?"

The lift of his spear was eloquent. There could be predators lying in wait—the boys had to have the best chance they could get.

"Go ahead. Take half the men with you and be careful. Yell if you see anything." Eidhal glanced at the sun. "I can give you the best part of an hour. Move ahead, but don't go past the crescent."

He sighed as they raced up the path to the crest, wishing he were with them, but command held duties and they could not be ignored.

"Sir! Could you tell us what to expect? Give us a hint?"

"What's your name, boy?"

"Clem Marish, sir. I—"

"You should have known better than to ask." Eidhal remembered him now. He had worn the yellow for a period, no blame in that, but blame enough now that he had broken the rule.

"Yes, sir. I know, sir. I'm sorry." Terrified, afraid of what was to come.

"Just stay calm," said Eidhal, quietly. Safe advice

which he must have received already. No father would remain wholly silent, despite the tradition. "Keep your head, stay where we put you and be resolute."

The boy nodded, unconvinced, and Eidhal remembered something else. An older brother who had failed to return—no wonder the lad was scared.

"Up," he ordered briskly. To delay now would be cruel. Fear was contagious. "Up and on our way!"

Beyond the crest, a fan of cleared thorn ran up a gentle slope which rose abruptly into a mass of slender pinnacles of jagged stone. They ran in an uneven curve for the distance of a mile, the remains of an old ridge which had been shattered and eroded in eons past. Rocks were heaped at the foot of the spires, clumps of grass and scrub clinging to the detritus. A section had been cleared—the high places of the ordeal.

Eidhal led the way towards them, walking straight, seeing the figures of Armand and his men looking small as they quested among the rocks.

Dumarest watched them come. He leaned against a pinnacle, the woman slumped at his feet. Iduna was close to exhaustion, her hair soiled, her clothing grimed, her eyes bruised hollows in the pallor of her face.

"Earl!" she muttered. "Earl?"

"Men," he said. "Men and boys." He added, comfortingly, "It's all right, Iduna. We're safe now."

"Safe? With animals like the Candarish?"

"With people."

He moved, feeling the nagging ache of bruises, of muscles overstrained. The laceration on his scalp was a festering burn. Despite his reassurance, he was being cautious. If these men were from the valley he had searched for, they could have a short way with strangers. A people who wanted to remain secret could not afford to arouse curiosity. He stepped behind the pinnacle as Iduna rose to stand beside him.

"Boys," she said wonderingly. "Why are they here, Earl? What are they doing?"

The party had halted before one of the cleared fingers of stone. As they watched a boy climbed it, reaching the top to cling awkwardly to the jagged summit. Once settled, the others moved away to another pinnacle well away from the first.

"Earl?"

"A rite," he said. "An initiation. Those boys will have to stay up there all night. They will have to stay awake, hanging on, wait until the dawn. They could be up there for days."

"But why?" She had spoken without thinking, too tired to correlate facts into an answer. "What is the point?"

"A tribal custom. Once they have passed the test, they will become men." Dumarest glanced at the party, the questing scouts. As yet they were unobserved. "We've arrived at a bad time."

"Will they kill us?"

It was possible. Strangers, in a sacred place, observers who did not belong. It would be better to hide, to wait until night. But even so, there could be guards and certainly there would be predators of one kind or another. Beasts waiting for tired hands to slip, young bodies to fall, easy feeding in this savage wilderness.

"Madness," she said, too numb to follow her question, to demand an answer. "To treat children like that. Why do they do it?"

To weed out the unfit, to test courage, to make manhood a prized estate. A crude method, perhaps, but one which worked. Dumarest had seen it before, tests by fire, water, the ability to go without food and to live off the land. A means to ensure physical stamina, to eliminate destructive genes from the line.

No small community could afford to carry the burden of the handicapped. No sensible culture would permit destructive variations in the gene plasm to survive.

Had Leon refused to participate? Running, a victim of his own terror? It was possible—if he had come from the valley which lay beyond. If the valley was Nerth.

"Earl!"

He spun at Iduna's cry, seeing a multilegged thing,

spined tail upcurved, mandibles champing. A scor-pion-like thing a foot long, which scuttled forward towards her foot. It squelched beneath the impact of his heel, but the damage had been done.

"Eidhal! Here!"

Armand came running, spear leveled, men at his back. Dumarest stooped, picked up two stones, fist-sized rocks which he held in each hand. He threw one to either side, waiting until they fell, their rattle distract-ing the guards. Then, as they hesitated, he stepped for-ward, hands uplifted, palms forward in the unmistak-able sign of peace.

Armand threw his spear. It was a slender shaft five feet long, the tip cruelly barbed. Sharp metal which glinted as it flashed, straight and fast towards Du-marest's chest. His hand dropped, caught it as he turned, continuing the movement so that he spun in a complete circle, running as he faced the man before him.

"Eidhal!"

Armand stepped back, caught his foot on a stone, and fell as Dumarest lunged towards him. He saw the face, tense, smeared with dirt and dried blood, the vicious tip of the spear flashing towards his throat. He felt the sharp prick as it came to rest touching his windpipe.

"No!"

"Hold!" Eidhal came running foward. "Don't kill him! You men there! Hold your spears!"

He halted close to Dumarest, looking at the man on the ground, the drop of blood showing beneath the point of the spear.

"Press on that shaft and you die! I swear it." His eyes lifted, saw Iduna, took her for a man. "Both of you die."

"You would kill a woman?"

"A woman?" Eidhal looked again, caught the swell of breasts beneath the stained tunic, the curve of the hips. "She too, if you kill Armand. You hold three lives in your hand."

Neatly put—and he meant it. Dumarest looked at

the ring of guards, the scared and wondering faces of
the boys yet to climb the pinnacles. They were well-
trained, not one had moved, and guards had remained
at their station.

"I came in peace. I showed empty hands, yet he
tried to kill me. Why?"

Armand swallowed as Dumarest lifted the spear
from his throat a little.

"I saw movement. There are predators—and you
wear gray."

The mark of a ghost, he was not to blame. Eidhal
glanced at Dumarest, saw his face, remembered the incredible speed with which he had avoided the thrown
spear. No ghost this, no matter what he wore.

One of the guards cleared his throat.

"Varg, the boys?"

A timely reminder, already shadows were gathering
in the hollows. Unless the initiation was canceled, they
would have to move fast.

"Continue. Split up the men and work at speed."
Again Eidhal studied Dumarest and the woman.
Strangers—and the rule was clear. But the boys would
be watching and, as yet, they were not men. "Where
are you from?"

"That way." Dumarest jerked his head as he stepped
back, still holding the spear.

"From there? The north?" Eidhal was incredulous.
Nothing human could have come from that direction.

"We were on a raft and had an accident. Three survived. One died when we were attacked by a beast."

Eidhal sucked his his breath as Dumarest described
it.

"A tirran! And you killed it?"

"Killed it and lived on its flesh." Dumarest looked at
the pinnacles, the young, watching faces. "Don't you
get them here?"

"Rarely. The last one I saw was years ago, and I
counted myself fortunate that it did not attack." Eidhal
looked at the pair with respect. "Here we get codors—
smaller, but just as vicious in their way." Too vicious,

but he did not like to think of that. And his duty remained to be done.

Down towards the valley, he decided. On the level place in the path. The boys would not be able to see the swift execution, and the bodies would have vanished by dawn. A pity, the man held strength, and the woman could provide healthy children. The rule was sometimes hard.

"You had best come with me," he said. "The boys must wait alone. Armand, your spear."

Dumarest retained it, looking from one to the other, judging distance. He could kill at least two, perhaps more, but if he fought now the end would be inevitable. And there could be no need to fight. He looked at Eidhal, the green he wore.

"A question, you will answer it?"

"Yes." A man, soon to die, should be treated with courtesy.

"I am looking for Nerth, have I found it?" He saw the blank expression and felt a momentary unease. Yet, if these were the Original People they would be reluctant to admit it. He said, quickly, "I come bearing a message from Leon Harvey. You know him?" Without waiting for an answer he produced the photograph. "I will give it to her."

There was a comfort in the Council chamber, as if time itself had been halted and trapped in the thick stone of the walls, the massive beams of the roof. Thick laminations of wood constructed with loving care. Signs of the ancients were on all sides, faces carved in timber which seemed to move and shift in the dancing flames of lanterns, to smile, nod and, sometimes, to frown.

A fantasy, Phal Vestaler knew. Inanimate things could not pass judgement, but if the stones could speak surely they would protest now. The thud of his gavel demanded silence.

"Gentlemen, you will please remember that you constitute the Council. We are not at festival, but at deliberation. Aryan, you may speak."

The man took his time. A skilled orator he knew the value of suspense and, thought Vestaler grimly, had much support from others less gifted.

"Aryan?"

"With respect, Master, I was assembling my thoughts." Rising, as custom demanded, so that all could see every play of expression Aryan cleared his throat. "The matter, as I see it, is basically simple. In fact, I am surprised that the Council has been convened to deal with it at all. Strangers are not allowed. All coming within the vicinity are to be destroyed. These two are strangers. Therefore, they should have been destroyed. Varg Eidhal failed in his sworn duty and should be punished." Pausing he added, "It is the rule."

Aryan knew the value of brevity in making a telling point. As he sat Vestaler said, "Croft?"

"I agree with all that Aryan has said." Croft, a small man, was eager to gain height by backing what he thought was the winning side. "The purpose of the rule is to ensure our isolation. Only by secrecy have we managed to remain apart and able to follow our ancient traditions. Once that is broken we will be subject to disruptive influences, the extent of which we can easily imagine."

"Usdon?"

"It seems that certain members of the Council are missing the point. We are not here to determine Eidhal's guilt, or to determine his punishment. Personally, I think the man acted with intelligent appreciation of the situation. The failure to kill is an error simple to rectify. The main object of concern, surely, is the man Dumarest and the message he claims to be carrying."

Sense at last, and Vestaler allowed himself to relax a little. Aryan and his supporters were evidence of a disturbing trend, an inward-turned concern with minutia and tradition. Blinded to the fact, though isolated, Nerth still existed in a larger universe than that of the valley.

Forgetting, too, the import of the message Dumarest

might bear. If he had met Leon, and if the boy had—but that was to hope for too much.

He glanced at the photograph lying before him on the table, the smiling face. Zafra's face, younger than it was now. He hoped that she would be spared more hurt.

"Master?"

It was Byrute. He rose at Vestaler's nod.

"Why can't we summon the man and demand that he gives us the message?"

"He insists on giving it to one person only."

"We could demand—"

"And be refused." Vestaler was sharp in his interruption. "We are dealing with no ordinary man. The mere fact of his survival is proof of that."

"He could have lied," said Byrute stubbornly. "There may have been no raft, no crash as he claimed."

"I have considered the possibility, but how else could he have reached us? And there is no denying the physical condition of both of them. The woman was so near to collapse that she had to be carried on a litter. Dumarest was in need of medical attention, and the state of his body proves that he had suffered in a manner consistent with what he says happened. To question him now would gain us little. Therefore, I propose that both he and the woman be granted a limited freedom until a final resolution can be made as to their fate."

The vote was carried as he knew it would be. The entire session had, in a sense, been a waste of time. Yet, the formalities had to be observed. A commune worked, not on dictatorial lines, but on common agreement. No one man could ever be allowed to become truly the master. The title he had won was by courtesy, not by right.

Later Usdon joined him, entering the Alphanian Chamber to walk towards the altar, to stand looking at what it contained.

He said, for no apparent reason, "Three failed, Master."

"I know."

"One of them was my daughter's son."

The extension of his line, a metaphorical continuation of his body. Vestaler remembered the boy. Sharp and bright and impatient to become a man. His pinnacle had been empty at dawn.

"He wasn't weak," said Usdon fiercely. "He wasn't full of guilt. There was no reason for him to have failed."

Vestaler remained silent. At such times there was nothing to say.

"I wish—" Usdon reached out and touched the artifact before him. "Now I wish that—" He shook his head, a man hurt, helpless to ease his pain. He found refuge in a greater hurt, a more poignant loss. "Do you think it possible that Dumarest can help?"

The odds were against it and yet, hope still survived. Hope, but Vestaler could only be honest.

"I doubt it, Marl." His hand fell to the shoulder of his friend. "I can't see how he could."

Chapter TWELVE

Dumarest stretched, remembering. There had been food and drink, hot water in which to bathe, a cup of something pungent, a bed in which to fall. And there had been pain, a searing agony in his scalp, hands which had held him fast, a voice which had murmured soft instructions.

His hand lifted to touch his scalp, the fingers resting on a patch of something smooth.

"Don't touch it," said a voice. "You will aggravate the wound."

Dumarest sat upright, looking at a room he barely remembered. Small, the walls of stone, the window heavily barred. A door of wooden planks held the grill of a Judas window. The bed was solid, the mattress firm, the covers of thick, patch-work material. Reds and greens and diamonds of yellow. Blue and amber squares, and triangles of puce, purple and brown.

"We had to clean and cauterize," said the voice. "The infection was deep."

She sat on a chair set hard against the wall, a position beyond the range of his vision until he turned. A woman no longer young, one with blonde hair held by a fillet of metal. The eyes were amber, the face strongly boned.

"I am Zafra Harvey."

"Leon's mother?"

"Once I had a son." Her voice was distant, as if she spoke of another life at another time. "You claimed to have something to tell me. A message."

"It can wait." Dumarest rose higher in the bed. He was naked. "Did you take care of me?"

137

"Yes, I am skilled in healing."

"A doctor? A nurse? How is Iduna?"

"Your woman is well. She was suffering only from exhaustion. Now that she has eaten and slept, she will be fine."

"She isn't my woman," said Dumarest. He looked at Zafra's face, seeing the mesh of tiny lines at the corners of the eyes, the aging of the lips, the neck. "How long has it been since that photograph was taken?"

"A long time. In happier days."

"Here?" And then, as she made no answer. "In the town? Do you often leave Nerth?"

"Nerth?"

"The valley. Do you?"

"We call it Ayat. No, we never leave."

The name they would use to others—and the woman had lied.

She said, "Please. The message?"

"Later."

"But Leon—"

"Your son?" Dumarest nodded as he caught her faint inclination. "What happened to him? Why did he run?"

"He is dead. We do not talk of him."

A symbolical death perhaps attended by appropriate ceremonies, his name stricken from any records there might be, his very memory erased. A name that should not be mentioned. A custom with which Dumarest was familiar, one with which he had no patience.

But she was a woman, a mother, and he had no reason to hurt her.

"I knew him," he said. "We worked together, traveled together. He told me of this place. He said that you could help me." A lie, but barely. The photograph had told him that and Leon had carried it. He added, gently, "I am sorry to tell you that he is dead."

She sat as if made of stone.

"What happened?" he urged. "Did he fail his test? Run because of shame?"

"The shame was not his. He wore the yellow, but

that was understood. But then, when the time came again, he was not to be found."

"He ran," said Dumarest. "But how? With whom?"

"None went with him."

"A raft? A trader?"

She made no answer and he knew he would gain no further information at this time. Rising he stood, fighting a momentary nausea, then moved to a table which stood against a wall. It held his things, the knife, the idol he had carried tucked beneath his tunic, other things, his clothes. They had been cleaned and dipped into something which had left a purple film. He rubbed it, seeing it leave a mark on his thumb.

"Gray is the color worn by ghosts," she explained. "Green, those who are here by right. The purple will save you from embarrassment."

"That's considerate of you." Dumarest picked up the knife and scraped casually at the idol. "Am I under restraint? If so, it will give me an opportunity to work on this."

"You are free to move at will among the houses and immediate fields. No work will be demanded of you. You may eat with the single men and widowers."

"No guards?"

"You will be watched. And now, if you please, give me the message you claim to have bought."

"You've had it, a part of it at least. Leon is dead. I thought you would like to know. He died bravely, a hero to those who knew him." An unqualified lie this time, but one which could do no harm and could give comfort. Dumarest followed it with another. "He died in my arms. He mentioned you and asked me to bring you his love. The rest of what he told me is for other ears than your own."

"Did he mention——" She broke off as if conscious that she was asking too much. That she could be abrogating the authority of others, demanding more than was her due.

"You were saying?"

"Nothing." Rising, she moved towards the door.

"Take care of your wound. If the pain should increase, let me know at once. If you feel fevered or dizzy, the same. It would be wise for you to conserve your strength for the next few days."

Good advice, and he might follow it—if he was allowed to live that long.

It was late afternoon, and Dumarest guessed that the drug he had been given had made him sleep for thirty hours or more. A long rest which he had needed, and now he was hungry.

He ate in a hut with a score of others, men who watched but said nothing. Not even the youngsters who, at least, must have been curious. The food was good, a steamed mass of beans and meat flavored with herbs. A pudding of nuts and honey, dark with small, crushed bodies. Insects perhaps, or seeds, or even maggots bred to give added protein. Dumarest ate without worrying about the nature of the food.

The meal ended with a mug of tisane, hot water which had been steeped with acrid herbs. A crude, medicinal compound, but one which apparently worked. The men he could see looked healthy as had the boys, the guards. He nodded at a familiar face.

"Hello. Are you one of my watchers?"

Varg Eidhal grunted, hesitated for a moment, then moved to plump down on the bench at Dumarest's side.

"You ate well," he commented. "That is good. A fighting man needs to build his strength."

"The boys, how many failed?"

"Three." Eidhal was grim. "Two who vanished and one who will be a ghost."

"Three—is it always that high?"

"Sometimes more, rarely less. Never is there a time when all return."

"And you don't mind?"

"It is the rule."

The rule, the law, the custom which governed their

lives. One of a skein of such regulations, and Dumarest could only guess at what they were.

He said, "If you are to watch me, you had better stay close. You can show me around."

A guide in more senses than one and, perhaps, an ally in case of need. A small hope, the conditioning of a lifetime would not be thrown aside in a moment, but Dumarest could not afford to neglect any opportunity.

The houses were interesting, strongly built, solid, patterned on those he had seen in the town. All carried some form of decoration, a bow, a bull, the design of a crab, others. From a smithy came the sound of hammering, a brawny man nodding as Eidhal halted in the open doorway.

"The spear-heads will be ready soon, Varg. Now I must fashion knives for the new men."

"Couldn't they wait?"

The smith grinned as he swung his hammer. "Remember your own time, Varg. Could you?"

A knife, the badge of manhood, edged and pointed steel worn proudly in the belt for all to see. Dumarest had wondered why he had been allowed to retain his own weapon. Now he knew.

They moved on, past houses closed and snug, others with open fronts in which women sat spinning, turning pottery, grinding grain into flour with the help of men who sweated as they turned the heavy millstones. A busy, active community in which all shared the labor and the reward.

Dumarest looked thoughtfully at a long, low, heavily-shuttered building which stood apart from the others.

"What is that?"

"The Alphanian Chamber."

"And that is?"

"The special place where ceremonies are conducted. Where the past is remembered."

Where records would be kept, and items rendered sacred by rarity and time would be housed. Alphanian

. . . alpha . . . a word Dumarest knew meant the beginning.

"Varg, what do you people call yourselves?"

"We are of Ayat."

"And?" Dumarest pressed the question as the man remained silent. "Are you the Original People?"

"I—let me show you the fields."

Not an admission, but admission enough. And yet, a mystery remained. The name, Ayat, a cover perhaps. But why had Leon claimed he came from Nerth?

The fields were well-kept, the rows of beans clear of weeds. Others held ripening grain, root crops, bushes yielding nuts and fruit. Domestic animals would be kept at the lower end of the valley. Dumarest watched as boys and young girls shooed away birds. Only when older, and puberty exercised its demands, would they be kept apart.

Eidhal paused as a man came shambling down the path. He was tall, big, shoulders wide beneath the drab gray of his smock. His face was vacuous, the eyes empty of intelligence, his mouth wet with spittle. The lips twisted into an inane grin as he halted before Dumarest.

"Give . . . you give . . ."

"He wants something sweet," said Eidhal. He rummaged in a pocket and found a dried fruit. "Give him this."

A splayed hand snatched the morsel and thrust it into the slavering mouth.

"That's all, Odo," said Eidhal as the hand reached out again. "Get back to your work."

"Give . . . you give . . ."

"No! To work now!"

"Odo want . . ."

"Odo will be beaten if he does not do as he is told." Eidhal was firm, but gentle. "Come on, now, back to work."

Dumarest stood to one side as the guard conducted the idiot back into the fields.

"A ghost," Eidhal explained as he returned. "A child who will never be a man."

"How did it happen?"

"It happens." Eidhal was grim. "Sometimes a boy grows in body, but not in mind. He is given every chance, as that one is there." He pointed to where a boy wore a yellow sash. "If a lad thinks he is unready for the ordeal, he is allowed to wait and no shame comes to him, or to his parents. If still he refuses, then he wears gray."

"Do many refuse?"

"In my lifetime, only one. He was sent to clear thorn and live in isolation. He died by his own hand."

"And Odo?"

"He was a bright lad, smart, keen and eager to become a man. The pride of all who knew him. I was on duty at the time. When dawn came, he was as you see him now." He added, bleakly, "It would have been better had he vanished."

An idiot condemned to a life of unending labor, castrated to avoid the continuation of his line, a man who had become little more than an animal. Despised, rejected, yet needed as an essential source of labor. A ghost.

And yet, Eidhal had been kind. Dumarest wondered if there was some relationship between them. It was more than likely; in any closed community blood-ties had to be plentiful. His son, perhaps, or the son of a sister, a cousin.

Kind—yet he would have been more merciful had he thrust his spear into Odo's heart.

Iduna was waiting as they returned. She ran forward, eyes anxious as they looked at the dressing on Dumarest's scalp.

"Earl! I was so worried. Your head?"

"Is fine. And you?"

She had lost the ghastly pallor of exhaustion. Her hair was a smooth russet helmet about her skull, the eyes clear, her skin carrying the faint sheen of health.

Like himself she wore purple, new garments which accentuated the lines of her figure.

She fell into step beside him, Varg Eidhal discreetly falling back. He, like them all, thought her to be Dumarest's woman.

"I've been listening," she said. "The woman talked when they thought I was asleep. Earl, they don't intend to let us go!"

"Did they say that in so many words?"

"They didn't have to. They talked of what I could do, and how I could be fitted into their community. They even speculated on a probable mate." Her voice carried undertones of disgust. "As if I had been a brood mare—good only to provide new children. My body used to increase their numbers."

And to provide a new source of genes. A cross would produce healthy offspring.

"Earl, what are we going to do?"

"We wait."

"For how long? Don't you understand what I'm saying? They spoke of me—not you. Whether I had any skills in weaving, pottery making, cooking, sewing of skins and cloth. All day they've been at it, questioning, probing, and never once did they mention you. They don't need you, Earl. I think they intend to kill you."

And, probably, her. The women had been gossiping, speculating, but the decision would not be theirs.

He said, "When they talked, did they mention a name?"

"A name?"

"That of this valley. Nerth."

"No." She was positive . . . "I asked them where we were and they wouldn't answer. But later, I heard one tell another that these were exciting times in Ayat." Her fingers tightened on his arm. "Earl, I'm afraid. We must escape before it is too late."

Escape into a wilderness without food, a map, or weapons. A short start with guards following, ready with their spears.

"We have to wait," he said patiently. "Take each thing as it comes. When our chance comes, we'll take it."

Empty words, but they seemed to give her courage.

"Wait," she said, brightening. "Yes, Earl, we must wait. But be careful. Don't let them hurt you. Promise them anything, do anything, but stay alive!"

An unexpected reaction, but he could guess at her latent hysteria. As a bell began to toll from the Alphanian Chamber, Eidhal edged forward.

"The curfew," he said. "And the summons. It is time for you to return to your quarters."

Them, but not others. Dumarest watched with interest as a stream of men and women made their way towards the enigmatic building. To participate in ceremonies, perhaps. To dwell on the beginning, if the name of the place meant what he suspected.

Later, he stood at the window of his room and looked at the stars. It was late and he could hear no sound of movement outside. The bars were firm and resisted his tug. The door was locked—a pail had been provided for natural needs. Only the roof remained.

Dumarest examined it as he stood on the end of the upturned bed. Thick rafters were crossed by thinner members, supports for the tiles which closed the building against the sky. With his knife he eased one free, set it gently on the floor, climbed up to remove others which he set outside. Within minutes he had a hole large enough to pass his body through, one which he could seal again from within.

A weakness in his prison, but those accustomed to regarding only doors and windows as a means of egress would have overlooked the obvious. And any prisoners, held in this place, would provide their own mental chains.

He jumped from the roof, landing as lightly as a cat, freezing, crouching to spot the silhouette of any guard against the sky.

He saw nothing. Either there were no guards, or they were on the other side of the building facing the door.

Rising, he ran quickly towards the Alphanian Chamber. It rested as a somber bulk beneath the stars, a fitful gleam of yellow light showing through the cracks of shutters, the join of the great double door.

It was held by a simple lock which yielded to the point of Dumarest's knife and he pushed one of the leaves open, slipping inside to close it behind him.

Turning, he looked at a museum. A church. It held something of both.

There were alcoves in which were painted designs fashioned of gleaming points, joined and surrounded by a tracery of lines. The depiction of animals, a woman, scales, a scorpion. Twelve of them, each faced by a thin stream of incense rising from bowls of hammered brass.

There were cases in which rested ancient books, strange artifacts, rocks and scraps of fabric. There was what could only be an altar, a high place set to the rear of a low dais. A painting of a woman, weeping. Another of fiery destruction. A third of something bright and wonderful emerging from a shattered egg.

The wall behind the altar was covered. The curve continued as it rose to merge into a smooth dome, a hemisphere broken only by the main part of the chamber. Beneath it, set in precise relationship to the apex of the dome, rested a squat construction which gleamed with polish.

Dumarest gave the place one quick glance, found it deserted of life, and moved around the walls studying the designs. The figures matched the mnemonic he had learned so long ago, the Ram, the Bull, the Heavenly Twins ... the Crab, the Lion ... The signs of the zodiac.

The thing for which he had been searching. And useless.

They were too abstract, the points which could only have been stars, too numerous and devoid of true relationship. He had hoped for set constellations easily remembered, signposts in the sky which would point the way to Earth. Instead, he looked at artistic impressions which could have no association with reality. Again he walked along the walls, looking, studying, trying to remember.

Had there been an archer in the skies? A man with the body of a horse drawing a bow? A woman emptying a pot of water? A pair of twins. A set of scales? A crab?

Not actual representations, but a pattern of stars, bright points which if followed with a marker would have left such designs. He remembered nothing, and such rudimentary portraits could not have been forgotten.

Impatiently, Dumarest moved to the books within the cases. The doors were closed and he forced one, leafing through a volume which smelt of mold. The pages were faded, stained. A record, as far as he could see, of names, births, deaths, matings. Another held details as to plantings, yields, types and varieties of vegetation. A third held rough designs of primitive, hand-operated machinery, grinders, scrapers, a potter's wheel.

He replaced it, closed the doors, moved towards the altar and the odd device it contained. Here, perhaps, he would find the answer. The lost but all important coordinates by which Earth could be found.

As he neared it he heard the sound of muffled voices, the creak of the opening doors. Dumarest looked upwards, searching for a place to hide, but the dome was unbroken.

To run was to fight. To fight at this time was to die. When Phal Vestaler entered the Alphanian Chamber attended by a score of guards, he found Dumarest kneeling before the altar, his head bowed, hands clasped in an attitude of supplication.

Chapter THIRTEEN

"Communing?" Aryan's voice held incredulity. "It isn't possible! He is unaware of the Mysteries." He sat at the table, annoyed, irritable at having been summoned so late. "It was a pretense, a ruse to save his life."

The truth, but Dumarest didn't like to hear it stated so dogmatically. He stood at the end of the table, uneasily aware of the guards at sides and rear. To them, he had committed an unpardonable crime. They would not hesitate to move in should the word be given. His life, he knew, hung on a thread.

And yet, he had an ally. From where he sat at the head of the table Vestaler said, quietly, "I told you what I had found. Nothing had been disturbed."

He had said nothing about the matter of the forced bookcase.

"And what if you hadn't sent for him? Discovered his escape?" Aryan flung the accusations like missiles. "And why did you send for him at all, Master?"

The question Vestaler had been expecting. Aryan would not take kindly to the intention of a private talk with Dumarest, but the man did not know what Zafra had reported. The hope her words had aroused.

A mistake, he thought, but one done now and impossible to ignore. Yet, if he hadn't sent for Dumarest, discovered him missing and gone with the anxiety of experience directly to the Alphanian Chamber—what then?

His rank and title, certainly. His position and all that

went with it. Shame and punishment, reduced to menial labor, shunned and despised as if he had been a ghost.

All that, if the man had lied. If he could not convince the others that he had entered the chamber for reasons other than to rob.

"Kill him!" snapped Aryan. "Kill him and have done."

"Wait!" Usdon's hand slammed against the table. "At least, let us hear what he has to say."

"He will spill lies," sneered Croft. "He knows nothing and—"

"You are certain of that?" Dumarest's voice rose to fill the chamber as he stepped forward, halting as his thighs touched the edge of the table. A calculated move designed to demand attention. "Do you think you are alone in the universe? The only ones who hold the ancient beliefs?" His voice deepened, grew solemn. "From terror they fled to find new places on which to expiate their sins. Only when cleansed will the race of Man be again united." The words he had heard from Leon, words he had heard before.

He fell silent, looking from face to face. Aryan, Croft, Vestaler, Usdon, Barog who as yet had said nothing. An old man who watched and voted, but who rarely spoke.

Now he said, slowly, "Do you claim to be one of our number?"

"Of your number, no. Of your following, yes. Do you think you are the only ones with such a creed? There are others on a host of worlds. Do you regard it as impossible that I am one of them?"

Croft said, sharply, "We are the true Original People. Others may claim that, but they lie. They use machines."

"You have a forge using bellows," said Dumarest. "You grind corn with the aid of a millstone, weave with a loom, fashion pots with a wheel. These things are also machines."

"But they do not use the demon of power."

"And so you consider yourself justified. A peculiar

interpretation of the creed. The cleansing mentioned has a deeper significance."

"You dare to condemn us? *You?*"

Aryan said, "You have still not told us why you entered the Alphanian Chamber."

To take the opportunity before it was too late. To learn what he could while he was able, but Dumarest couldn't tell him that.

"I am far from my people," he said quitely. "A stranger—and I know the rule. In my position, wouldn't you have done the same?"

A good answer, thought Vestaler, but Croft wasn't satisfied. He leaned forward on the table, still brooding over the imagined insult, the sense he had received of being corrected. Machines were the product of evil; because of them Man had become diversified. How could anyone who followed the creed believe otherwise?

He said, curtly, "I still think you lie."

"An easy thing to say when you sit in Council backed by your guards," said Dumarest. "Would it be as easy if we stood face to face outside? But then, of course, you don't believe in personal combat. Leon told me that."

"Leon Harvey! That renegade? That coward!"

"Coward?" Dumarest shook his head. "Call him what you like, but never call him that. Consider what he did. He, alone, left the valley and ventured through the wilderness to the town. A boy doing that and more. He found work, kept himself, gained money, traveled to another world. Coward?" His voice took on a chilling note of contempt. "From where I stand, it is you who are the coward, not he."

"Master!"

"You provoked him," said Vestaler shortly.

"But Leon—"

"We know what Leon Harvey did. There can be no excuse, that I agree."

"And yet this man defends him!" Croft was repulsive in his anger. "They are two of a kind. Has he come here to rob us further? A man who claims to have befriended a boy? That is enough to condemn him. I say he is a criminal and deserves to die. The rule demands it!"

The rule, always the rule, the iron barrier which Dumarest had yet to break. Croft was a fanatic as was Aryan, but hope could lie with the others. At least they had not demanded his life.

He said, slowly, "Have any of you ever stopped to think why Leon ran?"

"Can there be any doubt?" Usdon spoke before Croft could further vent his anger. "He could not face the ordeal."

"The ordeal," said Dumarest. "To climb to the summit of a pinnacle, to sit there during the night, afraid to sleep in case of falling, listening to the predators below, the things which climb and sting. A healthy lad should have no trouble in staying awake. A fit one to hang on. Agreed?"

Usdon nodded.

"Then why, always, do some fail?"

"Guilt," snapped Aryan. "Fear. A knowledge of their own weakness. A proof that they are unfit to survive."

"No!" said Usdon sharply. "My—" He broke off, unwilling to mention his own recent loss.

A reluctance Dumarest recognized. A fortunate circumstance which would back his gamble.

"We spoke of cleansing," he said to Croft. "You sneer at others who believe as you do, but who use machines. Use them, but are not dominated by them, that is the important difference. Power, in itself, can do no harm. It is like a spear which, in itself, is a useful tool. It is the man using it which makes it evil. A spear, a knife, a gun, all tools, all forms of power. Any form of power can be misused. The ordeal is a form of power. The power you have over the young. A power you have misused."

He heard the sharp intake of breath, the instinctive protest at what they considered to be an insanely unfair accusation. Bluntly he pressed on.

"A boy ran from the only home he had ever known. He left his mother, his friends, his people. He plunged into the unknown—and yet some of you call him a coward. You never even considered that he might have a reason. And none of you seem to care about the boys who vanish, or the ones who are found turned into ghosts. Do you want to continue sacrificing your youngsters? Do you enjoy the tears of their mothers? The misuse of your power?"

"It is a test," rapped Aryan.

"An initiation. We have always had it," echoed Croft.

Barog, more observant than the others, less blinded by pride said, "You misjudge us. We are not evil men."

"You know," said Usdon. He looked at his hands, they were trembling. Too late, he thought bleakly. No matter what happened now, it was too late. Sham was gone—nothing could bring him back. Nothing. And yet, others could be saved if Dumarest had not lied. If he could prove his accusation to be just. "You know," he said again. "Know what happens to the boys, what robs their brains."

"Yes," said Dumarest. "I know and I will tell you—for a price."

Iduna shivered as she stepped from the door of the house, a reaction caused less by the chill than the sight of armed men looming in front of her in the starlight. The waking had been abrupt, a touch and a whispered command, her demand for explanation ignored. Perhaps, now, she was to be taken to some secluded place, there to be quietly disposed of, speared to death and buried.

Varg Eidhal's voice was a rumbling reassurance.

"Don't worry, we mean you no harm. It is just that you are wanted in the Council Chamber."

"Why?"

"Just walk beside us."

To a mockery of a trial, questions which could have

no answers. A sentence which, somehow, she had to avoid.

She stumbled a little as she entered the warmly lit chamber. Eyes, accustomed to the outer darkness, unable to see detail immediately. Then she saw men seated at a table, more guards, the tall figure of Dumarest.

"Earl! What—"

"It's nothing serious, Iduna." He was, she saw, relaxed, apparently in command of the situation. She drew a deep breath of relief. "I just want you to answer some questions." He nodded to where Vestaler sat at the head of the table. "The truth now, there is no need to lie."

He watched the ring of faces as she verified what he had already told the Council. Yes, she had accompanied her brother on an expedition. They had crashed. He had died in the crash and their guide had also been killed. By a beast? Well, yes, in a way.

"In what way?" Aryan was quick to note the hesitation. He frowned as she explained. "So Dumarest killed him. Are you accusing him of murder?"

"No, the man was badly hurt, dying, in great pain. There was nothing else we could do."

"We?"

"He, Dumarest, he was merciful."

A type of mercy to which they were unaccustomed, and Vestaler frowned. Yet, the point was not worth pursuing at this time.

"Tell us of the Kheld."

"The Kheld?" She glanced at Dumarest. "Why, we, that is my brother, thought they could be found in the mountains. An ancient form of life native to this world, which at one time had threatened the town. My brother," she added, "was suffering from strain."

"He was deranged?"

"No."

"Deluded, then?" Vestaler rapped the table as she hesitated. "You must answer the question. Was your brother wholly normal?"

"Yes. It was just that he had this determination to find the Kheld."

"Did he?"

"No."

"Have you any proof, any kind of proof whatsoever, that such creatures exist?"

Again she hesitated, not knowing just what to say, wondering what the assembly was all about. To lie and perhaps damn herself and Dumarest, or to tell the truth and perhaps do the same.

"Shall I repeat the question?"

"No, that will not be necessary." The truth, Dumarest had said. For want of a better guide she obeyed. "No, I have not."

"You have never seen them? The Kheld, I mean."

"No."

From where he sat Croft said, harshly, "A lie. I knew it. Another to add to the rest."

A logical summation, but Usdon wasn't satisfied. A stubborn hope, perhaps. A confidence in the boy which had never been shaken. Sham could not have failed. There had to be an explanation.

Dumarest gave it.

"Iduna did not share my experience," he said. "She was asleep at the time. I told you that, but you insisted on questioning her."

"With reason," said Aryan. "Your story is preposterous. An invisible something which you heard, but did not see. The stuff of legends, stories to terrify children. If they exist, why haven't we seen them?"

"Or heard them?" said Croft, triumphantly. "Answer that if you can."

He was trapped, thought Vestaler bleakly. Dumarest had bargained well. His life and that of the woman, to be spared for the sake of his information, the proof. The information he had given, the lack of proof would snap shut the jaws of a trap of his own making.

"You haven't seen them," said Dumarest, quietly, "because if you had, you would have become a ghost. As for hearing them, perhaps you have. Think," he urged, "remember. You have all undertaken the ordeal. Did none of you hear a thin sound in the air then? A chittering? Feel an impression of menace?"

He waited for an answer, but it was too long ago. Even if they remembered, none would admit it. Perhaps with cause. To be the first to back his claim would be to share his implied guilt.

"The Kheld are old," he said. "Perhaps now very few in number. They must be an aerial form of life, and so would never enter the valleys. The updraft would be too strong. The pinnacles are high, ideally placed for the creatures to reach. On them you set boys, easy targets for such predators. They come, take what they need, leave without trace."

"If what you say is true, then why are not all the boys affected?"

A shrewd question, Barog was no fool.

"I said they were few," reminded Dumarest. "Perhaps they maintain a territorial area, perhaps each boy provides food for more than one. Frankly, I don't know. But I can guess what happens. The boys are lone, afraid, each a prey to his own fears and imagination. And then the Kheld draw near. I have heard the sound. It numbs, clogs the brain—and I am a grown man. A boy would be terrified. Perhaps the very emotion induced by the Kheld is what they feed on. That, or some form of nervous energy—again I am not sure. But there is a way to find out."

"And that is?"

"You are all grown men. Prove it."

Usdon sucked in his breath, quick to understand.

"Prove it," snapped Dumarest. "Do what you demand children do. Undertake the ordeal." His finger rose to point at Aryan. "You!" At Croft. "You!" At the others, one after the other. "Prove that you are men—if you dare!"

Eidhal was a boy again, a child who clung to the summit of his pinnacle and tried to forget all the rumors and inflated tales, the fears, the memories of

those who had undertaken the ordeal and had not returned. A young lad, alone and frightened, as he
watched the wheeling of the stars, heard the soft sough
of the wind as it rose from the valley.

An illusion, he was not a child and he was not alone.
Aryan sat on the finger of stone to his right, Croft
beyond, Dumarest to his left. Two other volunteers
from the guards further down, Usdon beyond them.

A bad place but he had insisted, insisted too that
there be seven of them, the smallest number to undertake the initiation. The others of the Council were admitted to be too old. Barog would never have managed
the climb, Vestaler had been overruled.

A scrabble and Eidhal kicked, a multi-legged body
falling to the ground. Trust the ilden to scent prey. A
nuisance more than anything else, but a sting could
burn, cause a hand to slip, a body to fall. Below, the
codors would be waiting.

He relaxed, forcing himself to ease an inner tension.
There was nothing to worry about. He had done this
before and remained unscathed. True, four others of
his batch had failed and another had turned into a
ghost, but that had been years ago. Yet, they had been
as strong as he. Had he survived only because of the
luck of the draw, as Dumarest had suggested? One of
those who had not been attacked by the mysterious
Kheld? Would he have survived if he had?

Odo, he had been strong too, a virile lad with a zest
for life, quick at games, the delight of his mother, the
pride of Charl. He had died a year later, slow to lift his
spear, wanting to find a clean end, perhaps. Lyd also
had not lasted long. She had mourned her husband and
then had gone to walk among the predators which had
taken him. Eidhal had followed her, too late. She had
died in his arms, his only sister—why was life so unfair?

He stiffened as he heard a faint sound. The wind? It
was possible. The soft breeze could play tricks with a
straining ear. He listened again, concentrating, hearing
a thin, high chittering which died as soon as it regis-

tered. A familiar sound, one he had forgotten, his skin prickling as he recalled the past. Even then he had not been sure, dismissing it as a figment of imagination, remembering the advice he had been given.

"Remain calm, keep your head, be resolute." Advice he had passed on.

A puff of wind and again the weird, eerie sound, this time accompanied by another. The soft impact of climbing boots, the rasp of a human breath.

"Varg—can you hear it?"

Dumarest, clinging to the stone, looking upwards, his face dim in the starlight.

"I'm not sure. I—"

"Come down. Quietly. You can handle the predators?"

"Yes." Glad of action Eidhal climbed down the high pinnacle, stood at Dumarest's side. "What is it?"

"Over there. Where Croft is. Don't make a noise."

He moved to the right, soundless, Eidhal like a shadow at his side. He had expected the ground to be thick with codors, but none were in evidence. A chittinous body crushed beneath his foot, proof of their stealth. The things were normally wary.

"Listen!"

Dumarest had halted, looking upwards to where Croft sat perched on his finger of stone. The man was visible only as a blur against the stars. A blur which moved as the air filled with a faint stridulation, a chittering which grew stronger, lowered, seemed to hover over the dim shape, to engulf it.

Croft moaned. It was a sound barely louder than a sigh. A release of breath from constricted lungs, a prolonged exhalation. The chittering increased in volume and then, abruptly, stilled.

"God!" Eidhal felt his stomach contract, his skin crawl as he looked upwards. "What the hell's happening?"

On the pinnacle, something was feeding. It was diaphanous, a thing of gauzy membranes which caught the starlight and reflected it in wispy shimmers. A web of near-invisible filaments which could ride the wind, falling as it condensed, rising as it extended. A web which was formed of a diffused kind of life, alien to human experience.

"Croft! We must—"

"No!" Dumarest held the man fast. There was nothing they could do—and a point had to be proven. "He's gone," he said. "It's already too late. If he doesn't fall and kill himself, he'll be a ghost."

Chapter FOURTEEN

"Croft." Vestaler shook his head, conscious of his guilt, his relief that it had not been Usdon. Wine stood on the table and he poured himself a measure, sipping, his eyes thoughtful as he stared over the rim of the goblet. "Why?" he demanded. "Why Croft?"

"He was afraid," said Dumarest. "His own fear killed him."

His own terror, the sweat of fear perhaps, attracting the Kheld to its scent. Usdon's face darkened as he remembered what he had seen. It had been a mercy the man had fallen, crushing his skull as he landed, to lie helpless for the predators.

They had been denied their prey. The body was taken, buried now with all honors. A ceremony Croft had deserved. By his death, he had saved the lives of others. No longer would the ordeal be held in the high places. The initiation would be changed, young lives saved, the uneasy presence of the ghosts eliminated for all time.

Usdon poured wine, handed Dumarest a goblet, lifted his own in salute.

"For what you have done, we thank you," he said with formal courtesy. "May your life among us be long and pleasant."

The next barrier was to be surmounted. He and Iduna were safe, but still confined to the valley. A problem to be solved, but Dumarest said nothing as he returned the salute.

The wine was strong, rich with flavor, comforting to his stomach and easing his fatigue. The journey, the vigil, the return—and his full strength had yet to return.

"How did you know?" asked Vestaler. "Did Leon tell you?"

"No, he betrayed none of your secrets. But what must have happened was obvious. He was curious and must have sneaked close to the high places to watch the ordeal. He saw something, or heard something, and it frightened him. He wore the yellow to gain time and, when it ran out, he could do nothing but run." Dumarest lowered the empty goblet. "In his way, he was very brave."

"You liked him," said Usdon with sudden understanding. "He reminded you of someone, perhaps."

Of himself when young, traveling, working, moving on. A little bewildered and unsure, a stranger in a constantly changing world. But Leon had lacked the one thing Dumarest possessed, the luck which had enabled him to survive.

There, but for the grace of God, went I! A sobering thought.

"What I can't understand is how you managed to escape the Kheld the first time you experienced them," said Vestaler. "When you were on your journey."

"There were four of us," said Dumarest. "We were close. Chaque and I were awake and able to give each other strength. And I have met odd life forms before."

"And you are not prone to fear," said Usdon. "Your courage saved the others."

"Perhaps." Dumarest helped himself to more wine. "But I think Jalch saved us. He was dreaming, experiencing a nightmare, and he woke. Perhaps his thoughts, his hate—who can tell?"

"Yet you went to the high places knowing what could happen. The act of a brave man." Again, Usdon lifted his goblet in salute. "You and your woman will breed fine children. They, in turn, will add to the strength of others."

"She is not my woman."

"Not of the Original People?" Usdon frowned, then shrugged. "It is not important. She can be indoctrinated into the mysteries, taught the things we know, the past which has to be remembered. It is unusual, but it can be done. We owe you that and more."

There would be a house and a position, rank which would gain in stature as the years passed. There would be work to engage his hands and mind, boys to train, men to teach. He would tell them stories of other worlds and expand their horizons, far beyond that of the valley. Given time he could change their ways, introduce machines, encourage trade. Give them life.

Already they were too inbred, young faces bearing a similar stamp, lines of weakness lying close beneath the surface. Fresh blood would revitalize them, his own and that of others. The mountains could hold minerals and gems, the predators could provide skins and furs. Even the Kheld could be snared and sold to zoos. A worthy task for any man and here, maybe, he would come as close as he ever would to home. To Earth.

A temptation. A snare loaded with enticing bait; authority, respect, security, the power to manipulate lives, to guide the destiny of a people. Iduna.

She entered the chamber as if at a signal, coming directly towards him, her hands extended, features radiating pleasure.

"Earl! I've been so worried! Thank God you're alive and well!"

"And you?"

"They kept me within a house. There was a loom and some of the women tried to teach me how to use it. Earl, it's not for me."

He said, flatly, "They say that we have to stay here. You will have to weave, bake bread, make pots, do what the other women do. Mate with me," he added. "Bear my children."

"Earl!"

"Does the prospect horrify you?"

"No, why should it?" Her eyes were candid as they met his own. "If we have to, then we must."

"Your body against mine," he said deliberately. "Hot as we mate, your womb filled with child, growing, swelling, later to feed the new life. And not just once, Iduna, but many times. We shall eat together, sleep together. Your body will provide my pleasure, my hands—" He broke off, eyes narrowed, searching. "You do not object?"

"No." She swallowed, then managed to smile. "Of course not. You are a fine man, Earl. No woman could ask for better. We can be happy here, you and I. The valley is a nice place, the people kind. When—?"

"Now! Today!"

"You mean that tonight—?" Again, she swallowed. "But why the hurry? Earl, you must give me a little time, a few days at least. My brother—I can't forget Jalch so soon."

"He was your brother, Iduna, not your husband. I shall be that."

"Yes, Earl, of course. Even so, I need a little time." Her laugh was strained. "You don't understand. I—you will be the first. Please, Earl! Please!"

She sagged as he nodded, her relief obvious. As she left Dumarest said, dryly, "As I told you, she is not my woman."

"But she will obey." Vestaler had watched from where he stood against a wall. "She must obey. There is no alternative."

"I disagree," said Dumarest quietly. "We could always leave."

"That is impossible. No one can leave the valley!"

"No?" Dumarest looked from one to the other, from Usdon to Vestaler. "Like Zafra, you lie. Men left the valley to go searching for Leon. He saw them and they frightened him. That's why he took passage on the first vessel he could find."

"He—"

"Ran," interrupted Dumarest. "We know why, but he did not leave empty handed. He took three things with him. A map which he had to have in order to find his way from the mountains. Something of value which he could sell in order to obtain passage money—what was it?"

"An ancient seal," said Usdon bitterly. "Made of precious metal and gems. It has been with us since the beginning."

"And the photograph," said Vestaler. "The one you brought with you. It is of no importance."

Dumarest said, quietly, "I wasn't counting the photograph. There was something of far higher value. A safeguard in case he should be caught. With it, he could bargain for his life."

"The Eye!" Usdon turned to Vestaler. "Master, he is talking of the Eye of the Past!"

He knew! He had to know. For a moment relief made Vestaler giddy, so that he had to clutch at the table for support. The brooding, the regret was over. Now, at last, he could sleep easily at night instead of spending endless hours in self-recrimination. He should have known, suspected. But how to even imagine the possibility of such an event?

For a boy to act so! The very concept was incredible.

He said, fighting to control the tenor of his voice, "You know? He told you?" And then, as Dumarest remained silent, he shouted, "If you know where it is, man, tell us! I beg you!"

"I will," said Dumarest. "The moment I reach the town."

The price—always there seemed to be a price. First, his life and that of the woman. Now, the demand to leave the valley, to travel safely under escort to the city. To be taken to the field where ships landed and departed for other worlds.

A danger. A thing contrary to the rule—yet how could he refuse?

Vestaler felt that his world had overturned, conscious that he dealt with a man accustomed to things beyond his experience. One who had early learned to take advantage of every chance life had to offer, to gain any edge in order to survive.

"The Eye, Phal," urged Usdon. "The Eye of the Past."

The most sacred object they possessed. One which had been stolen and now, by an incredible series of events, could be regained.

If Leon hadn't met Dumarest. If he hadn't died. If Dumarest himself had died in the crash, or in the mountains—surely fate had guided him.

Or—had he lied? It was possible. Vestaler strained his mind, trying to remember if he had given any clue, any hint which could have been caught, inflated and bounced back as a boy would bounce a ball against a wall. The photograph? Three things, Dumarest had said. Had the photograph been originally one of them, the story changed as he dismissed its importance? Had Usdon spoken too quickly? Provided the essential clue?

Vestaler groped for the wine, filled a goblet with trembling hands, wine spilling as he lifted it to his mouth and gulped it down. How to be sure?

"The Eye, have you seen it?" Dumarest remained silent.

"How large is it, then?" Usdon was more devious. "You can see that we need proof of what you say."

"It isn't very large—and you need no proof. I will deliver it once I reach the town."

So it was on Shajok! Again Vestaler reached for the wine, halting his hand as it touched the jug. Now was the time for a clear head, and he regretted what he had already taken.

"So it is in the town," he said. "You could tell us where it is and, when we have recovered it, you will be free to leave."

"No."

"You doubt my word?"

"It's my life," said Dumarest harshly. "Too many accidents could happen on the journey. We do it my way, or not at all."

An impasse, but Usdon had a suggestion. "The woman, are you willing to leave her behind?"

"To join me later? Yes."

A possible way out, yet would Dumarest really care if she joined him at all? A chance they had to take, and there would be armed men accompanying him with firm instructions to kill if he should attempt to elude them, or fail to do as he promised.

"Very well," said Vestaler. "Let us make the arrangements."

Iduna glanced at them as they left the house. She stood several yards away, facing the end of the valley away from the mountains.

She stiffened as Dumarest touched her.

"Earl! You promised—"

"To leave you alone and I shall. I'll be leaving soon. You will follow in a few days."

"Leaving? No, Earl, you can't! You mustn't leave me here alone!"

"You'll be safe, Iduna." His voice hardened at her expression. "There's no help for it. It has to be this way."

"You could wait another few days."

"Wait for what?"

"For—" Her eyes moved from his face, focused on the sky, grew alight at what she saw. "For that, Earl. For that!"

A raft which dropped quickly to the ground, to settle close. A raft which held two figures dressed in flaming scarlet, one holding a laser, both adorned with the great seal of the Cyclan.

Chapter FIFTEEN

Hsi dominated the Council chamber. He stood like a living flame at the end of the table, the acolyte at his side. The cyber's voice was a careful modulation, only the words held an implacable threat.

"I have a device buried within my body. Should my heart cease to beat a signal will be sent and received by those to whom I belong. They will know when and where I died. If it is in this valley, then total destruction will follow. Every man, woman and child, every plant, every animal will be burned to ash."

"You wouldn't dare," said Vastaler. "You haven't the power."

"It would be a mistake for you to think that," said Hsi evenly. "I have no concern for you in this valley—once I depart you may continue your life as before. My only interest lies in Earl Dumarest."

And he had him, finally caught, unable to run, prevented from killing by his concern for others. A weakness which no cyber would be guilty of. Hsi felt the warm satisfaction of mental achievement, the only real pleasure he could know.

"You followed me."

"Of course, Once you had been located on Tradum, your capture was inevitable. Did you really think you could continue to elude the Cyclan?"

"The boy," said Dumarest. "You found him."

"A simple prediction. He was an innocent, a dreamer who tried to get close to you by the use of a name. Nerth—there is no such place, but the name was close enough to another to arouse your interest. He must have picked up a rumor, or overheard you talking, the details are unimportant. The drug sold you by the apothecary was useless. A harmless sedative. Your use of the raft to gain access to the field was ingenious."

Dumarest said, dryly, "I was in a hurry."

"With reason. You would have been caught within the hour. As it was, Captain Shwarb knew what to do."

Bribed, as every other captain had been bribed.

"You told the boy what ship I was on," said Dumarest harshly. "He came aboard after I did. And you paid Dinok and the engineer to lie about his planet of origin. Leon had to be killed, of course—you red swine!"

"He was expendable."

"You sent me to Shajok," said Dumarest bitterly. "Offered me a bait I couldn't refuse. I should have guessed."

"Every man has a weakness," said Hsi. "And no man can have the kind of luck forever which has saved you so often. The accident of chance and circumstance which, coupled with your quick thinking, has enabled you to escape the Cyclan until now."

"Why did you wait so long. You know where I was headed. You could have had a reception committee waiting at the field."

"Time was against us. Ships few and far between. And precautions were taken."

"Yes," said Dumarest. He looked at the woman. "What did they promise you, Iduna?"

"Earl?"

"At first I suspected Chaque. Your brother was too obvious and the Cyclan are never that. Chaque was a last-minute replacement. Then, when he was dying, he tried to tell me something about you. What happened? Did he see you using a radio in your tent one night? Spot something else when he was watching you undress? Threaten to betray you unless you saw things his way?"

"I don't understand." She looked at him, puzzled. "Earl, what are you saying? We were to be married.

You know I wanted to be with you. You know that I love you."

"Like hell you do!"

She cried out as his knife flashed, cut, the material of her blouse falling apart to reveal high, full breasts held and molded by delicate fabric. He cut again and drew the severed band from around her waist. A thin belt, barely an inch wide. Metal showed at the cut ends.

"A signal beacon." Dumarest threw it to one side. "You knew help would be coming. That's why you insisted on waiting. But you're a bad actress, Iduna. You can't pretend what you don't feel. And you can't mask what you do feel. That's what made me certain."

Her recoiling when he had touched her, her expression when he had described their future, the deliberate crudity and detailed anticipation.

"And Chaque?"

"He was an animal," she snapped. "He wanted to use me."

"And you suffered him. You had no choice. Why, Iduna? Did the Cyclan promise to heal your brother? Was Jalch that important to you?"

"He was insane! A fool!"

A man who, incredibly, had been right, but Dumarest didn't mention that. Nor the kiss she had given him, the proof that she sometimes could act.

"What then?" he urged. "To give you the body of a man?" He caught the betraying flicker of her eyes. "So that was it. To rid you of the female flesh you wear. The body you hate. A pity, you could be beautiful."

"Beautiful!" She almost spat, her face ugly, distorted by anger. "A thing to be used by men for their own, selfish pleasure. God, why was I born a woman? I can do anything a man can do, and do it better than most. Yet because I have this—" her hands touched her naked body, "I am considered to be an amusing novelty. A toy. Can you guess what it is like to hate what you are? I would do anything, anything to be a man."

She was insane, he realized, like her brother obsessed. Yet, where he had been proven right she was

demonstrably wrong. Her conviction of inferiority was
a product of the paranoia which had turned her into a
sexual cripple.

He said, cruelly, "Are you so sure they can deliver
what they promised?"

"What?" Iduna glanced to where the cyber stood,
tall, impassive, the acolyte watchful at his side. "They
must! They will!"

"Why should they? You heard what Hsi said about
Leon, the boy was expendable. And, now, so are you.
You've done your job, guided him to me. From now
on, you are unnecessary."

His voice was a hammer beating at the weak fabric
of her mind, feeding the paranoia she shared with
Jalch.

"Can't you see they have used you? Promised more
than they can deliver? Played on your weakness? You
will never be a man, Iduna. The life you hoped for is a
dream."

"No!"

"Tell her, Hsi. Be honest. A cyber has no need to
lie. You can't do what she wants and you know it. Tell
her!"

Hsi said, evenly, "The thing can be done given time.
You know that."

"Time?" Iduna faced him, taking a step forward,
madness in her eyes. An animal poised and tense,
ready to spring, to tear and kill. "You lied," she said
thickly. "Damn you—you lied!"

"Ega!"

The acolyte fired as she sprang, the beam of the laser
hitting her between the eyes, searing a hole through
skin, flesh and bone into the brain beneath. One shot
and then the acolyte was falling too, equally dead, the
hilt of Dumarest's thrown knife a red-rimmed pro-
trusion in the socket of an eye.

"Earl! No!"

Dumarest ignored Usdon's shout. As the blade left
his hand he sprang, hand lifted, stiffened, falling to
slam against the cyber's temple. As the man slumped

he tore at the wide sleeves of the robe, ripped free the laser he had known would be there.

"You've killed him!" Vestaler stared his horror, shocked by the sudden death which had entered the chamber. "The valley!"

"He isn't dead. Now fetch Odo and hurry!"

His stirred, sitting upright on the table on which he had fallen. The blow had barely stunned, and he felt no pain from the bruised flesh. For a moment he remained silent, looking at the two dead figures, at Dumarest now alone in the chamber.

"That was unnecessary," he said. "You would not have been harmed."

"No?"

"Your life is important to us, as you must know."

"My life, yes," admitted Dumarest. "But your definition of harm and mine are not the same. You could have burned my legs, my arms. Because my brain would remain undamaged, to you there would have been no harm. My brain and the knowledge it contains."

"Knowledge we must have. It is ours, stolen from the Cyclan. The affinity twin was developed in our laboratory."

"Old history," said Dumarest. "Possession, now, is all that counts. I have it and you do not. That makes me the master."

"A fool. Give us the correct sequence of the fifteen units and you will be rewarded. That I promise."

"Money, a place in which to live, luxury, good food, men to obey me, security—for how long? No, Hsi. We both know that I remain alive only because you need me. Once you have the secret, I will follow others. Derai," said Dumarest bitterly. "Kalin, Lallia—I have reason to hate the Cyclan."

Hate, an emotion unknown to the cyber as were all others. Love, fear, pity, greed, ambition, hope—all things which weakened lesser men.

"Mistakes have been made," admitted Hsi. "You

were an unknown factor incorrectly assessed. Those who failed have paid the penalty. But I shall not fail. I have you and you cannot escape."

"No?"

"You cannot kill me, your concern for the inhabitants of this valley prevents you. You cannot escape—my raft will respond only to my personal control. You could cripple me, but what will that serve? No, Dumarest, for you this is the end. The very people you protect will hold you prisoner in order to save their lives. Logic, surely, dictates that you accept the inevitable."

The summation of known facts which, to the cyber, led to only one conclusion. Dumarest would not kill, he could not run, he could only wait. Soon now he would be held in a secret laboratory, his brain probed, the essential sequence of the units discovered.

"Logic," said Dumarest. "The cold calculations of a mechanical mind. Well, perhaps you are right. We shall see."

He moved down the chamber, turning, fumbling beneath his tunic, fingers busy at his belt. When he turned, he held something in his hand. A small metal tube, the walls thick, strong.

"The affinity twin," he said. "You wanted it—you may have it."

"The sequence—"

"Is something else." Dumarest raised his voice. "Odo?"

He stumbled as he entered the chamber, Vestaler at his side, Usdon at his rear. Catching his balance to stand, he was drooling, eyes blank as he looked at the dead.

"Odo want," he mumbled. "Give Odo something nice."

Dried fruits which he stuffed into his mouth to stand chewing, spittle dribbling over his chin. Vestaler was uneasy.

"Earl, what do you intend to do? If you kill the cyber, we shall all die. If you do not—"

"He could have lied," said Usdon. "Did he?"

"No."

"Then, if he dies, we shall all be destroyed?"

"Yes."

"So it is in your interest that I be kept alive," said Hsi evenly. "More, that I be obeyed. Dumarest must be held fast, firmly bound and guarded. You will do that. He will be placed in my raft, together with men to watch him." He rose from where he sat at the end of the table. "I shall leave immediately."

Usdon glanced at Vestaler. "Master?"

"We have no choice," said Vestaler bitterly. "I am sorry, Earl, but we have to do as the cyber says."

Do as he had predicted, but the achievement was minor, the mental pleasure small.

Dumarest said, "Wait. There is another way."

"The valley——"

"Will not be harmed. That I promise." The metal tube parted in his hands, revealed two small syringes, one tipped with red, the other green. "Red," he said, showing it to Hsi. "The submissive half of the affinity twin."

"So?"

"You wanted it—here it is!"

Dumarest moved with a sudden release of energy, crossing the distance between them before the other realized what he intended, the cyber's hand lifting, touching the syringe now buried in his neck.

"No! You——"

"Have solved the problem," said Dumarest harshly. "Think about it, cyber—if you can!"

If the man could still think at all. His intelligence was trapped by the biological unit now nestling at the base of his cortex, totally divorced from the control of his body, the machinery of his mind. Aware, perhaps, as if in a dream. Lost in a timeless limbo.

"He isn't dead," said Dumarest as the others moved towards him. "Think of him as a cup waiting to be filled." He moved again, this time towards Odo, the green syringe plunging into the idiot's flesh. A moment and it was done.

"Odo!" Vestaler looked at him, the limp body supported by Dumarest's arms. "I don't understand," he said blankly. "What has happened?"

"Odo is asleep," said Dumarest. "You must take good care of him. He can be fed, washed and kept warm, but he can do nothing for himself." He lowered the heavy body to the ground.

"And the cyber?"

Hsi looked at his hands. He turned them, peering, mouth open, slack in the skull-like contours of his face. His eyes were empty, vacuous, the blank windows of a deserted house. From his lips came a thin drone.

"Odo wants . . . give Odo . . . Odo good . . ."

The intelligence of the idiot now dominant in the body of the cyber. The transfer of ego which was the magic of the affinity twin. Dumarest handed him a scrap of dried fruit.

"What happened?" Usdon was baffled. "I saw—what happened?"

"They changed," said Vestaler. "The cyber became Odo. Is Odo. Earl!"

Dumarest caught the note of fear, recognized its cause.

"You have nothing to worry about," he said. "Hsi's body is alive and well. No signal will be sent and no retribution turned against you. I'll take him with me when I leave in his raft. The body of the acolyte will be dumped in the wilderness."

Dumped, but his robe retained. Wearing it Dumarest would accompany the apparent cyber to the city, take passage on a vessel, leave the pathetic creature on some far world. He would be found, taken care of—the Cyclan looked after its own.

But before that happened Dumarest would have vanished, moved on, losing himself in the infinity of space.

Vestaler said, dully, "And the Eye? The Eye of the Past? I suppose all you said about that was just a lie in order to escape."

"No," said Dumarest. "It wasn't wholly a lie."

He had left the idol in his room, going to fetch it, returning with it in his hand to the Alphanian Chamber where the others waited. For a long moment Dumarest looked at the designs, the scraps of various materials in the cases, the books. Then he faced the others where they stood before the altar, the idol in his hand.

"Leon carried this," he explained. "A hobby, perhaps, but I never saw him work on it. The material is the same as was used by the woman potter for whom he worked in the city. A convenient substance to cover something he might have wanted to hide. Something he could have stolen."

"The Eye?" Vestaler's hand trembled as he touched the crude depiction. "In there?"

For answer Dumarest lifted it, smashed it hard against the stone floor. It shattered, lumps splitting apart, fragments flying, a heap of granules dull in the yellow light. Among them, something gleamed.

"The Eye!" Vestaler's voice was a shout of joy. "The Eye of the Past!"

It was small, round, a lens of crystal filled with a blur of formless designs, flecks of color blended in wild profusion. Vestaler snatched it up, wiped it clean, tears of thankfulness running over his withered cheeks.

The Eye returned! Once again in its rightful place! The impossible achieved! His mind swam with a giddy relief.

"What is it?" said Dumarest. "What is it for?"

The man had a right to know—without him the ache would still exist, the hurt remain. Fate must have directed him, the ancient ones striving in their immutable fashion, How else to explain it?

Usdon said, quietly, "Phal, he has earned the right."

The initiation, the safety of the valley—yes, he had earned the right. More than earned it, yet tradition must be maintained.

Vestaler said, formally. "Usdon, do you propose that Earl Dumarest be shown the inner mysteries?"

"Master, I do."

"And you, Earl Dumarest, soon to leave us, do you swear that never, ever, will you betray to others what you are about to see?"

"I swear."

"You are with us, if not of us. We of the Original People accept you. Now come with me, watch and be humble."

Vestaler turned and approached the enigmatic machine set in the floor beneath the dome. He stooped over it as Usdon moved softly about the chamber, extinguishing the lanterns. When only one remained at the far end of the chamber, he came to stand beside Dumarest.

"Now," said Vestaler. "Witness the glories now lost to us. The past we must remember."

He touched something and, suddenly, light and color filled the dome.

A pattern.

A scene.

A part of ancient Earth.

Dumarest knew it, felt it, sensed that it could be nothing else. It was all around him, streaming from the machine, light directed through the Eye, the lens which held holographic images.

A park, neatly cropped grass, trees, birds which hung like jeweled fabrications. In the foreground, a soaring monument of weathered stone. An oblisk with a pointed tip.

A blur, another scene. A bridge which seemed to float above a river, strands like those of a spider's web. In the water, the shapes of assorted vessels.

The faces of solemn giants carved on the side of a mountain.

A vast canyon.

A great waterfall.

Oceans, ice, deserts, endless fields of ripening grain. Massive pyramids, cities which stretched to the horizon, soaring buildings which reached for the sky.

Scene after scene, each filling the dome, all building to a culmination of awesome majesty.

One planet to have held so much!

Earth!

But now the world Dumarest had known. Here were no signs of dreadful scars, the arid bleakness he had known as a boy. No gaping sores—this was a world at peace, bursting with energy and life, a planet in its prime.

He blinked as the scenes ended, darkness closing in, momentarily disoriented.

"The things we must remember," whispered Vestaler. "Our ancient heritage, lost to us because of heinous ways. One day, when we are cleansed, it will be ours again."

Dumarest turned to move away, felt Usdon's grip on his arm.

"Wait. There is more."

A flicker and the dome shone with stars. Blazing points overlaid with names and numbers—Sirius 8.7, Procyon 11.4, Altair 16.5, Epsilon Indi 11.3, Alpha Centauri 4.3 . . .

Signposts in the sky! Dumarest stared at them, impressing the data on his memory. Names and numbers which had to be distances. A relationship could be established by a computer, the common center determined, the modern coordinates found.

"Earl?" Usdon was beside him, his voice anxious. "Your face—is anything wrong,"

Dumarest drew a deep breath. The raft was waiting, soon he would be on his way. Now, it would be only a matter of time before his search was over.

"No," he said. "Nothing is wrong."